AMBER FANG
Revenge

ARTHUR SLADE

AMBER FANG

Revenge

ORCA BOOK PUBLISHERS

Copyright © 2019 Arthur Slade

All rights reserved. No part of this publication may be reproduced or transmitted in any form or by any means, electronic or mechanical, including photocopying, recording or by any information storage and retrieval system now known or to be invented, without permission in writing from the publisher.

Library and Archives Canada Cataloguing in Publication

Title: Revenge / Arthur Slade.
Names: Slade, Arthur, 1967– author.

Description: Series statement: Amber Fang ; 3

Identifiers: Canadiana (print) 20190068728 |
Canadiana (ebook) 20190068744 | ISBN 9781459822757 (softcover) |
ISBN 9781459822764 (PDF) | ISBN 9781459822771 (EPUB)

Classification: LCC PS8587.L343 R48 2019 | DDC jC813/.54—dc23

Library of Congress Control Number: 2019934025
Simultaneously published in Canada and the United States in 2019

Summary: In the third novel of this series for teen readers, a vampire librarian hunts down a secret organization.

Orca Book Publishers is committed to reducing the consumption of nonrenewable resources in the making of our books. We make every effort to use materials that support a sustainable future.

Orca Book Publishers gratefully acknowledges the support for its publishing programs provided by the following agencies: the Government of Canada, the Canada Council for the Arts and the Province of British Columbia through the BC Arts Council and the Book Publishing Tax Credit.

Design by Gerilee McBride
Cover image by Christian McLeod/Stocksy.com
Author photo by Black Box Images/Jerry Humeny

ORCA BOOK PUBLISHERS
orcabook.com

Printed and bound in Canada.

22 21 20 19 • 4 3 2 1

For the librarians.

One
BLOOD IN THE SAND

MY FIRST GOAL was to not spill any blood in the sand.

Placencia is a small fishing village in Belize with an odd mix of tired, quaint buildings and fancy new tourist digs made of faux palm trees and glass. The beach is not much more than a strip, yet it's beautiful, and there's a lovely view of the Caribbean Sea. The tourists were generally happy, the locals had genuine smiles, and the weather was calm.

It was a shame I was hunting a murderer here.

A shame but totally necessary. A girl has got to eat.

The sand on the beach squished pleasurably between my toes. The palm trees waved pleasantly above me. The air was stinking hot, but I'd taken the precaution of slathering on an SPF 45 suntan lotion, from my feet to my forehead. The sun won't kill me, but vampires burn easily—well, the pale ones do. I wore a black one-piece swimsuit and a lovely straw hat.

The man I was going to eat had just lowered his chiseled and tattooed body onto a red towel. Those tattoos would be used to identify his corpse later. He was Grigoriy Belyakov and, as you can guess by his name, he was Russian. Not ballet-loving Russian. But more the Kalashnikov-firing, vodka-loving type. Someone has to be the stereotype.

He was also a high-level employee of ZARC Industries and the key to where my mother had been taken. There were at least twenty people—from journalists to envoys to bystanders—who had been killed by this hit man. And he obviously was experiencing no regrets for those murders. In fact, he'd just finished several regret-free sangrias before heading to the beach.

He was exactly the type of man my mother, Nigella Fang, would approve of—for eating, that is. She had taught me to have only ethical meals. It is how vampires should behave. Apparently, she and I are in the minority as far as vampires are concerned. The rest of my relatives will eat any human they can sink their teeth into. They are so gauche.

I'd followed Grigoriy from his cabin and had been keeping my eye on him over the last twenty-four hours. As far as I could tell, he was alone here, which suggested he was truly on holiday. He adjusted his sunglasses and, lo and behold, pulled out a book to read. I squinted, but I couldn't tell what the title was.

So he wasn't completely horrible. The fact he was a reader meant I'd be extra careful to not mess up the feeding part of this venture. That's my deal with murderers who have enough taste to be bookworms—no messy death!

Not that I am a naturally messy eater. But sometimes mess happens.

I chose a shady spot several feet away, spread out my own towel, sat down and watched him closely. I even separated his heartbeat from all the sun-slowed heartbeats of the sunbathers around him. The breeze carried his scent my way, a pleasant cologne.

I watched.

And I watched.

The crashing waves and the heat were sleep inducing, and I hadn't been sleeping well since I'd seen my mom at a ZARC compound in Canada three months earlier. I thought I'd rescued her by grabbing a huge egg, but inside it, waiting like a scorpion, I'd found my father instead.

It was kind of like finding a dog turd inside a Christmas present.

Dad was still in that egg at a military base in Montana. Dermot had rejigged the dials and revamped the life-sustaining systems, and we were pretty sure my father would continue to live. I wanted Dad to stay on ice. Permanently, if necessary.

Dermot has been helping me track down Mom, but his resources have shrunk like Cinderella's pumpkins at midnight. He is basically all that is left of the once-powerful League, a group of do-gooders who wanted to rid the world of enemy agents. But they have been mostly wiped out by several ZARC hit teams.

Dermot was watching me watch the murderer. By that I mean Dermot was observing the scene with a drone that hovered at a very great height above this beach. I could just hear its rotors. No one else should be able to.

Our big break came three weeks ago when I received a text that said: **From one book lover to another. A gift.** The image of Grigoriy was texted to me, along with a PDF of his hit-man background and a copy of his travel plans.

Is that you, Agnes? I'd texted back. There had been no reply.

There was also no way to trace the origin of the text. The number was just 000000000. There was no conceivable way for anyone to have my secret phone number other than Dermot. Yet the text had still arrived. Nothing Dermot did—and he went all geeky on it—could find the source.

I was certain the text had come from the Returns—the ninja librarians who had rescued me from my sister's clutches. Even the thought that such a thing as ninja librarians existed still seemed ludicrous. But I'd seen their glinting dart guns and deadly accurate crossbows. Their official name is the Preservational Librarians Guild, and their goal is to preserve human knowledge and civilization. But they also have a policy of not interfering with the day-to-day world.

Still, I was pretty sure the text had come from the one ninja librarian who'd disobeyed their policies to give me information about Mom's location. Agnes. I could still see her dark, friendly face. I'd only said a few words to her.

But she knew me intimately. She was a Fanger—apparently there is a faction of librarians who follow my exploits using metadata and information sweeps and…well, who knows what. But they call themselves Fangers.

I still blush when I think of that. I have *fans*!

Fanger fans!

I was certain the reasons behind the text would come clear once I'd eaten Grigoriy.

Two blissful hours passed. I read. Snoozed with one eye open. The drone hovered.

My current read was *Life of Pi*, which seemed perfect for the beach—it was easy to fall into a novel about a boy trapped on a boat with a tiger when I could hear the waves only a few feet away. My only complaint was there wasn't enough bloodletting in the book. I found myself identifying with the tiger far too closely.

I must have snoozed with both eyes closed. When I opened them again, *Pi* was in the sand and Grigoriy was gone.

But it was a beach, and he'd left tracks, so I followed them. Oddly enough, I could tell that he'd walked right past me—dangerously close—but that could have been because the beach was so crowded and he'd been forced to take that path.

He had wandered over to one of the open bamboo huts set up with tables for Ping-Pong, foosball and other games for the tourists. The one he'd chosen had a pool table, and I heard the *crack, crack* of balls smashing into each other. I spotted him leaned over the table, sizing up his next shot. He seemed to be almost angry at the balls.

Death would soothe that anger.

I scanned the surrounding area to be sure no one was watching or nearby. Four posts held the roof above the table, and the walls were only hip high—the rest was open air. The walls would block any action once I had him on the ground. And I didn't need much more than two minutes to feed.

He was facing away from me, so I sneaked up the stairs without making a sound and slipped in behind him. He began to turn, perhaps had sensed my presence, but I clamped my hand on his shoulder and flipped him onto his back so hard that it drove the air out of his lungs, and the balls on the table popped up and down. I landed on him, with my knees on either side of his chest.

He snarled something in Russian and reached out with his meaty arms to choke me but was surprised when I grabbed them and easily pushed them back down. I licked my lips and noted that there was an octopus tentacle tattooed around his neck. The rest of the octopus, presumably, covered his back.

"We'll be conversing in English," I said. "Get it?"

He narrowed his thick eyebrows and replied, "Yes. I speak English."

"Good. You work for ZARC, right?"

"ZARC? Vhat is this ZARC?" He smiled as he said this.

"Don't play games. You're only half as clever as you think. You have information I need, and you'll give it to me. Now."

"Vhat information do you be needing?"

"There is a woman in your care, Nigella Fang. Do you know her?"

His smile widened. "Ov course, she's big bride."

"Bride?"

"Pride, is dat da word?"

"Pride?" Jesus, we were doing an Abbott and Costello routine.

"Prize," he said finally. "Big prize. I don't like your English words."

"Well, you won't like this either," I said, pressing my right knee into his chest. "I want you to tell me exactly where she's located. I need to find her."

"Dey know you are looking for her. You will not find her. You vill die."

"Thanks for the vote of confidence," I said. I pushed my knee even harder into his chest. "Anyway, you're here to help." He tried to get up, and I slammed him down. "I don't want to be testy about it, but I will break things. Things that are part of you."

"I've had everyting broken," he said.

Oh, that would make it harder to threaten him. And I didn't know if I could truly torture someone by snapping fingers or pulling off extremities. But as far as a comeback, all I came up with was, "You've never been questioned by a vampire. I'll go all medieval on your ass."

Grigoriy chuckled. I was starting to hate this man. He just wasn't taking me seriously enough.

Then... footsteps.

I snapped my head to the side, expecting to find an accomplice with an AK-47. Dermot was watching from a drone, but he was at least three minutes away if he ran fast.

Our visitor was a pale-skinned woman in an orange bikini. "Oh, sorry," she said.

I slipped my hand over Grigoriy's mouth so he couldn't talk. He bit me, but I didn't pull my hand away.

"I haven't seen him for months," I said, adding a conspiratorial wink. "I just couldn't help myself. He looks good enough to eat." She grinned, gave me the thumbs-up and backed away.

We were alone again.

I yanked my hand away from his mouth. He'd actually drawn blood. "Don't bite me! I'll bite *you*."

But in that moment of distraction, he had grabbed my shoulder and, in an impressive wrestling move, he shifted me to the side, slammed me down and somehow got on top of my back, forcing my face into the sandy floor.

I twisted my head, because it's always important to see your opponent. Grigoriy was grinning and perfectly at ease. He reached quickly into his hair and pulled out a long filament that glittered slightly. It had two little knobs on either end.

What the hell?

Its purpose became clear when he put it around my neck and began to twist.

A garrote. He'd somehow tied it into his short hair. Nice trick that, I thought, as I began to choke.

Two
THE UNVARNISHED TRUTH

I PANICKED AND SNAPPED my head back, but Grigoriy was pressing me down with his knee and pulling hard, managing to cut off the blood supply. He'd cut off my neck if he yanked hard enough.

I realized Dermot would be seeing none of this struggle because the roof would block his view. This had been a stupid place to launch my attack.

I tried to elbow Grigoriy and missed, then attempted to throw him off like a bucking bronco, but every movement just tightened the thin, seemingly unbreakable noose around my throat.

Seemingly unbreakable. That was the key. With a sudden flash of inspiration, I reached up but didn't grab the garrote because it would only cut my finger. Instead I drew my nails across it.

They are sharp as swords, but the wire didn't snap. I tried again, my thoughts going black. Nothing happened.

The third time, I caught the wire perfectly, and it snapped. Grigoriy fell back. I sucked in a deep breath, and my thoughts returned.

And with them, action.

Grigoriy launched himself at me, hands out. I took both his arms, slammed him to the floor again and then pinned him down. And I went for the neck.

"Drink my blood, no answers for you," he said.

"We'll see about that," I said. My throat was raw. "People talk more when they're closer to death."

"I von't talk. Never. Ever."

He tried to use some sort of rolling move he'd likely learned in the KGB. But I'm fast, and I found his gloriously big carotid vein with my teeth, and his blood burst into my mouth. I could taste the sangrias! The paralytic agent delivered by my teeth immediately did its work to make him sleepy. His struggles stopped. His body and his blood had been warmed by the sun, and something about being under the shade of palm trees made it taste better. It's funny the things you notice when you're feeding: everything slows down, including his heart and mine, which beat in slower and slower syncopation with his.

But I didn't want to kill Grigoriy. Not yet. I needed to, of course—he was my monthly feed. Feeling drowsy, I slowly pulled away. Looked. Two perfect holes. Not a drop of blood spilled. Damn, I was good. And he was a reader, after all.

"Grigoriy Belyakov, wake up," I said.

We were in somewhat new territory. I usually feed without an interrogation, but Dermot had done a few quick tests on the paralytic agent I injected into my meals and discovered there is a compound in it that is similar to truth serum.

So we'd cooked up a theory that people would be easier to interrogate once I'd sucked out a good portion of their blood.

"Grigoriy Belyakov, you will tell me the truth," I said, doing my best Svengali impression. "Awaken and tell me the truth."

His eyes slowly opened. A dim bulb of awareness appeared in them.

"Truth?"

Maybe this would work. "Yes. Where is my mother, Nigella Fang?"

"She's dead," he said very slowly.

My heart stopped beating. My chest grew tight. "Dead?"

"Dead veight," he said. Then he was silent, as if he was done explaining everything.

"What do you mean?"

"No eggs. No eggs." He now slurred out a wet, slobbery chuckle. "Dead veight. Dead experiment."

At first I thought he was hallucinating, but then it became clear what he meant. "She's not fertile, you mean."

He nodded aggravatingly slowly. Mom being infertile was not good news. Anthony Zarc had intended to weaponize her reproductive system for his biological military weapons.

But if she was of no use to him, that meant he could dispose of her at any moment.

"She's cheese," Grigoriy added. "Cheese. Cheese."

He was going bonkers. At least it was in English. Then my brain clicked again, remembering what cheese is for.

"She's the cheese in a mousetrap. To draw me to ZARC."

Grigoriy nodded slowly. "Smart mousie," he said. And he sounded slightly more awake now. Could the paralytic agent be wearing off already?

"Where is she? You will tell me."

He nodded. "In occupation room on experimental level."

"I assumed she was in a cell, but where is it, which continent?" I almost shouted this.

"Da red one."

"The red one? What country, I mean?"

"Da big cheese one."

"France? Italy?" Who the hell made cheese? And why did I have to play a guessing game? He was a smart bastard and obviously getting his faculties back.

"I can vink on my own now," he said, grinning. "Ha. I vink. I vink."

It was becoming clear that there wasn't any way to get the goods out of him. Perhaps he had been trained in some sort of anti-truth technique. "I'll eat you now," I said. And I darted down to finish my feed.

But just as my teeth touched his neck, he whispered, "I feel regret. English word. Regret."

"You what?"

"I feel regret. Sadness. I should not have done dose things I did. Dose murders. It was horrible. Dose people I killed. I am bad. I will repay da world with love."

Oh, sweet Jesus! One moral rule my mother drilled into me was to never, ever consume a murderer who feels honest regret. And there was no way to be certain this wasn't honest regret.

"Why would you say that?"

"That is vy I'm here on beach. To understand. To find my regret. Inner peach."

"Peach? Oh, peace." Crap. I was starving. And yet I couldn't kill him.

"So sad. So sorry for bad deeds. Would cry but tear ducts were removed by ZARC."

"Do you really feel regret?" I said.

"Yes. Yes. Yes."

I pulled away. He got up. He was surprisingly spry for someone who'd lost so much blood. He took a few steps and paused to lean on the pool table.

"I can't believe it vorked," he said when he was a few steps away. He was a little unsteady from all the blood loss. And he was obviously a little delirious too.

"What worked?"

"Dey said you had a moral code. So dat's vy I said it."

"So you *don't* feel regret?"

"Not one big bit," he said with a proud smile.

I was on him in a flash. I left his body under the table.

Three
MYSTERIOUS HEADGEAR

TIME WAS OF THE ESSENCE NOW, since Grigoriy's corpse would be discovered soon. I went directly to his cabana, looked left and right, then shoved open his door, snapping the lock. I stepped inside. It was a small room. So he didn't have horribly extravagant tastes. A bed was in one corner. His suitcase on a luggage stand next to it. Everything was neat.

Then the floor creaked behind me. I spun around to find Dermot with a sheepish look on his face.

"Sorry, Amber," he said, putting up his hands. "I forget how jumpy you can be after a feeding."

"I may have to put a bell on you," I said.

Actually, his shirt was louder than any bell. It was a red-and-purple Hawaiian number that could be spotted from the space station. Dermot had gained a few pounds in the last few months, but he still looked slightly emaciated. The veins on his arms stood out enough to make him appear like something halfway between a junkie and a weight lifter. He was as pale as a Victorian prince, a sign that he'd spent too much time staring at computer screens in battleships or underground bunkers. Whatever was in my sister's paralytic agent was being beaten, or at least held at bay, by the cocktail of drugs and supplements he'd been taking—and his augmentations.

Still, he continued to be somewhat handsome.

"You did well," he said. "Though you have a red line along your neck."

"Garrote. Sneaky Grigoriy hid it in his hair. The bruising will heal."

"Were you able to get anything out of him?"

"Only blood," I said.

He nodded, and we got to work searching Grigoriy's room.

I found another book. It was *Anna Karenina* in the original Russian. Would wonders never cease? If I didn't have all his blood sloshing around in my stomach, I could have had a conversation with Grigoriy about which Russian novelist was the greatest.

Well, no regrets about that. He was still a murderer extraordinaire.

We looked under Grigoriy's bed and found three knives—sharp-looking pig stickers meant to skewer, yet thin enough to hide in your sock. Obviously he couldn't fit them in his bathing suit. I guess the garrote in his hair was enough to make him feel safe.

Dermot had opened his suitcase on the bed.

"Five pants, seven shirts, twelve undershorts," Dermot said. He happened to be holding the man's undershorts at that time.

"You taking an inventory? Or wanting to try those on?"

"No and no. He was going to be here for a longer stay—these are clothes that are easy to hand-wash and hang dry. Perfect for traveling. That means he wasn't going to be reporting in for a week or two, and ZARC won't know he's gone. That gives us a head start."

"That's exactly what I was thinking," I said. It wasn't. In fact, none of those details had crossed my mind. But I didn't want Dermie to feel he was outthinking me. He has a quiet way of gloating that I really loathe.

"But head start to where?" I said.

"That's our biggest problem. We have no idea what information will be here. Keep looking."

We did. In the washroom. Nothing. In the waste bin. Nothing. I even sliced up his pillow with my fingernails. Nothing. Well, there was a lot of foam.

With each passing moment I grew a little more antsy. Someone could come across Grigoriy's body at any moment and scream bloody murder. And I had been spotted with him by one person. I also didn't know whether the Belizean police were as, um, relaxed as their fellow citizens. Or if they would descend on Placencia in helicopters and block all the exits with armored trucks. I really didn't want to find out.

I picked up the book again and flipped through the pages.

"What are you looking for?" Dermot asked.

"Oh, a diagram. A map. A gun. Whenever I watch a movie, the spies find their clues hidden in a book. Open a page and there it is."

"Looks like a typical paperback."

I shook it. "Well, the binding is good, at least." My Library Binding Methods class had been one of my favorites. I loved putting old books back together. It meant another two or twenty years of knowledge coming out of the book. Take that, you fragmenting hard drives.

Dermot opened a dresser drawer we'd somehow missed and found two mysterious clues waiting there—a ski cap and a pair of leather gloves.

"Lambskin interior with Thinsulate," he said. "Good to minus twenty."

"So he came from a cold climate. Siberia?" I shivered at the thought of traveling there. I still hadn't warmed up from my trip to Antarctica.

Dermot shrugged. "It really could be any northern climate, but this at least suggests he flew from that place directly to here." He opened the ski cap and shook it as if he were checking it for dandruff.

A business card fluttered out of the book and landed at my feet.

A card! How old style.

I picked it up and found an address in Uppsala, Sweden. Someone had written a phone number on the back.

Dermot took it from me, briefly touching my fingers as he did so. "Well, I guess this is all we have to go on."

"It's enough for me," I said. "Besides, it's a win-win. I've never been to Sweden."

Four
THE LAND OF THE SWEDISH COOK

THE ADDRESS ON THE CARD was in a neighborhood of Uppsala where the houses and apartment buildings were sunshiny yellow and light blue. I was reminded of Iceland. These Nordic cultures certainly weren't shy about bright colors. There was a bravery in that. When I returned to the drab browns, metallic grays and light greens of North America, it would be boring.

Oh, and the building at that address turned out to be an abandoned bowling alley called Latitude Dude. Bowling! I just couldn't imagine that the same Vikings who'd climbed aboard their longships and crossed the waters to lay waste to England, France and other countries would ever settle for bowling. But, like Icelanders, the Swedes exude peacefulness these days. Perhaps bowling is the closest they come to being aggressive. Except for their ice-hockey games.

Dermot had used his burnable phone to find our lodging on Airbnb. He'd rented a second-floor apartment with a large window that gave a nice view of the bowling alley. The main room was furnished with a futon, tables and shelves that all looked like they were straight from IKEA. The one noticeable exception was a six-foot chest freezer right in the middle of the room.

"What's in there?" I asked.

"Dead bodies," Dermot said, and he looked serious. But when I opened it, all I found were twenty freezer bags full of deer meat and a lot of icy buildup.

"It looks like it could hold a whole reindeer. Do you think we're renting from hunters?"

Dermot shrugged, and I closed the freezer. Poor humans! Vampire meals are always warm, and no preparation is necessary.

There was also a tired, old TV in the corner—perhaps from the '80s. I turned it on and was surprised that it still worked. All I'd learned of Swedish culture was from watching reruns of *The Muppet Show*—the Swedish Chef is one of my favorite characters. Thankfully, most of the men in Sweden don't look like him.

The apartment had two bedrooms. Each had a single bed. And each had a side table and matching analog clocks. The duvets were orange. Cozy and clean. But the size of the beds made it clear that the landlords didn't want any hanky-panky happening on their premises.

Not that there would be any. That was guaranteed.

Dermot set himself up in an observation station next to the window—by that I mean he moved a chair over and pulled out some fancy binoculars and watched the building. The place was closed. No one went in or out.

I sighed. This was the boring part of being an assassin. The waiting. Plus, there'd been a seven-hour time difference between here and Central America, and I was feeling it. I collapsed on the futon and put my feet up. I had digested most of Grigoriy's blood and lost the twelve pounds I'd gained from him within the first twenty-four hours after dining. I'm sure any diet guru wishes they had that sort of weight-loss success.

I sighed again.

Dermot looked at me. "Do you want something?"

You, I almost said. But I couldn't figure out how to say it as a joke. "I'm just wondering how you are. I'm sorry I slept so much on the flight."

"I'm fine. How are you?"

"Jeez, you sound like a robot when you say that. I mean, how are you since my sister bit you and you had that bad reaction to her paralytic agent and nearly wasted away to nothing. That's what I'm asking. You look better now. Do you feel better?"

He set his fancy binoculars down. "Yes, Amber. I feel a lot better. The wasting is, well, on the run. If I was to put a number on it, I'd say I was back to about 60 percent of my previous health level."

"God, you talk like such a dweeb sometimes! Are you still convinced your fancy-dancy augmentations saved you?"

"Yes. I am."

"You're always a little vague about them. Exactly what happened?"

"The League altered my DNA. So my reflexes are faster. They altered my face, since it was damaged in the accident."

"You mean when Hallgerdur, your ex-girlfriend, shot you." We'd been over this event before, and it was curious how he always called it an accident. "She did shoot you in the face, right?"

"Yes. The first shot anyway. The second was in the chest."

"She really, really didn't like you."

Dermot was running his hand along his skull, as if feeling for where the bullet had hit him. There wasn't a sign of the damage anymore. "She did have feelings for me once. But obviously those feelings changed. And the League changed me. Altered my structure. And my brain."

"Your brain?"

"Well, part of it was gone."

I think I'll file that under *Holy Shit!*

"Don't worry, Amber. It was only a negligible portion of brain. And the League scientists were able to grow it back. Most of it. But I lost things. Like... memories. Of my parents. Of my childhood."

"Oh, Dermot. I'm sorry."

"I'm not." He was looking at his hands now, as if inspecting them for dirt.

"You mean it was that bad of a childhood?"

"No. I'm not sorry because I can't remember a moment from that part of my past, so I am not able to be sorry it's gone. It's as if it never existed."

"It existed. It was real," I said. I thought of all the memories I had of my mother. Of her reading to me. Tobogganing down a hillside in North Dakota. "Either way, I'm sorry."

"It's partly why I want to help you find your mother. Because at least I can help you with your memories."

I must say, I wanted to hug him. Not a feeling I often have for humans. "Do you ever want to see your parents?"

"Someday. If they're alive, that is. Yes, someday."

I wanted to say more. But that was all I had. My energy was at a low ebb. It took all my will to stand and walk over to him and pat his shoulder. He reached up and touched my hand, then lifted the binoculars.

"You should sleep," he said. "Assassins need their fifty winks."

But I swear I saw a tear in his eye before it was covered by the binoculars.

I chose the closest bedroom, undressed and threw myself under the covers. I was out within seconds. I dreamed of the Swedish Chef. A very odd dream. There was a lot of Muppet stuffing and blood in it.

Hours later I opened my eyes and had the oddest yearning—for Dermot to be beside me. I rolled over and found myself face-to-face with a pillow. Ugh, I was getting soft.

I dressed and went out into the living room. Dermot was still sitting there, his spy glasses glued to his face.

The TV flickered with an old Clint Eastwood movie— *The Hanged Man*. Dermot hadn't turned up the sound. I put my hand to my throat, which still was a little rough from the garrote, then moved my hand down to my heart.

Clint Eastwood always reminds me of my mother.

She was his biggest fan and had forced me to watch every movie he'd been in. As a kid I'd loved to say, *You've got to ask yourself one question: Do I feel lucky?*

My mother would finish with, *Well, do ya, punk?* Then we'd laugh. He was our guilty pleasure.

Mom went to Clint Eastwood's house once when we were living in California. She sneaked into his room and watched him sleep. All night. She left before he awoke, but not before stealing one of his white undershirts.

As I said, she was his biggest fan. She was impressed that he didn't snore.

I shook my head, banishing the memories.

"Anything happen?" I asked Dermot. I was not certain he hadn't moved in the last few hours.

"There are five signals in there."

"Signals?"

He held the glasses in the air. "These are heat sensitive. Five people are sitting around a table and talking. I did not see them enter from this side. Obviously, we can't watch the other side. Though they could have come from underground."

"Male or female?"

"Four are male, judging by their size. But that's not always for certain. One is female."

For some reason, I thought of my sister, Patty. I got an arctic chill and an odd sense of longing. Like I still wanted to talk to her.

Which was insane, since the last time I'd seen her she'd wanted to take out my reproductive system lock, stock and barrel—fallopian tubes, uterus, et cetera—and plant it in some sort of egg-making machine they called Lilith. It hadn't sounded like an operation I'd survive. Nor did she seem to care.

And yet, when we'd talked on the ship before that, she'd been perfectly sisterly. We'd bonded.

Well, until she'd tried to kill Dermot by sucking out all his blood. And stabbed me in the hand with a spear.

Obviously, I was conflicted about dear sister Patty.

"What are you thinking about?" Dermot asked.

"Oh, nothing," I said.

"It won't be your sister in there," he said.

Could he read my mind? Oddly, guessing my thoughts was something my mother had often done. Had I spent enough time with him that he was starting to sense how I thought?

"I know that," I said. "She's not with ZARC. But they do have their share of femme fatales."

"Yes," he said. And this time I was certain he was thinking of his ex-girlfriend—Hallgerdur of the unerring shot. That made me nervous. She could be in a building two miles away and sending a carefully aimed bullet our way. I wondered which one of us she'd choose. Me first, since I was tougher, was my guess. I stayed out of the sight line of the window.

"Who do you think they are?" I asked.

"Honestly, Amber, I have no idea. I'm used to having reams of agent-collected data funneled to me before any decisions are made. But I'm blind, really. These five have been talking for hours. At one point it got heated—someone was shaking a fist. But other than that, I know nothing. This could be a meeting of high-level ZARC operatives or a group of teens playing Dungeons and Dragons."

"Dungeons and Dragons?" I said.

"You know, D&D? The role-playing game?"

"Yes. I know what it is. But really—why would that come to your mind?"

"It was meant to be funny."

I snorted. "It shows your nerdiness. It's unseemly."

He rolled his eyes. "Anyway, we'll only learn more if we go inside."

"Do we draw lots?"

He gave me an *Are you serious?* look. His face was still pale, and honestly, he wasn't as strong and full of bustle as he'd been when I first met him. I had this feeling that if we ran a few laps he'd be winded.

"I'm kidding," I said. "I was built for this. And I kinda like bowling. Except for the shoes. Hate those stupid shoes."

It took several minutes to get outfitted in one of the League's patented tactical outfits, which was basically a black synthetic suit that fit me like a second skin, hid my biorhythms and pheromones, and had a few pockets for keys, C-4 explosives and ammo. I felt stronger in the suit. And more professional.

When I came out of the room, Dermot gave me a look I couldn't quite read. Almost like he liked what he saw.

"Go get them," he said gruffly. He spoiled it all by adding, "But be careful."

"They're the ones who will have to be careful."

Then I was out the door, down the stairs and out onto the street, moving fast as a shadow.

Five
UGLY SHOES, UGLY CUSTOMERS

USUALLY I GO IN THROUGH THE ROOF. It's kind of a cliché for me now. I've climbed into prisons that way. Secret Antarctic fortresses. Even a McDonald's (that involved doing a bit of vent diving to surprise a mafia guy in Boston—I smelled like French fries for a week). So I decided to switch things up a bit. I walked toward the front door of the bowling alley.

"What are you doing?" Dermot squawked in my earbud.

I subvocalized, "Don't worry. I've got this covered."

And I did have it covered. You see, once I was near the building, I could track their heartbeats. So I knew where my enemies were located in the bowling alley, and none of them were even near the front. I opened the door slowly and was pleased to discover it was unlocked and had been recently oiled, so it didn't squeak. I slipped inside.

Damn bowling shoes were all over the front entry! Stacked up on the walls, strewn across the floor. They were all the same bad bowling-shoe colors and sizes you'd find in North America. It was as if there had been a stampede, and the last act of the crowd before going outside was to kick off their shoes. I nearly tripped over a particularly gaudy red-and-orange specimen.

I took in my surroundings. There were several lanes to my left, and the balls and pins had been spread out all over the place. It could have been any American bowling alley except for the foreign beer bottles dipslayed along the wall. People bowling and drinking seems dangerous to me, but humans are odd that way.

The heartbeats were in what I assumed was the café/bar area just out of sight.

The ceiling was, to my horror, suspended tile, so I couldn't sneak across it without the tile coming apart around me. That only left the floor. The carpet had been laid in the '70s and perhaps last vacuumed during that disco era. I crouched down behind a counter and crept toward my targets.

As I got closer, I realized the five were arguing—barking back and forth in loud voices, and I guessed it likely wasn't over who had the more up-to-date D&D manual. All the talking was in a guttural language that my ear placed as Russian, although I wasn't an expert. I imagine there are James Bond-type spies who would recognize the language or exactly which corner of Russia their enemy is from. Not moi. I am an experienced eavesdropper, but there really isn't much point if they aren't speaking English.

Glass broke. A tense silence followed. Then came rich and somewhat warm laughter. I sneaked past another collection of ugly shoes and wormed my way behind the bar. I was now just several feet from them.

"You don't need to get that close," Dermot said in my ear.

He was so loud that I did an involuntary shudder. His voice was not supposed to travel past the earbud, but I didn't trust the technology. "I only want to get a good sniff of them."

"Your nose that good? You hadn't mentioned that to me. I know it is a vampire superpower."

Actually, Mom was a better sniffer than I am. She said some vampires are as talented as bloodhounds at tracking down a scent, but my nose is only about twice as good as a human's. Perhaps there is training I could take to improve that skill.

"Let me do my work," I subvocalized.

Truth was, I didn't know what to do next. I didn't want to leave without any sort of information at all. Even their names would be something. Or I could follow one of them home ... if they ever left. But their grunting conversation soon made me grow sleepy.

Then one of the men shouted, "Hector!"

No one made a peep for several seconds.

My heartbeat started to speed up. This was finally a word I recognized—a name. Hector, of course, is the AI that Anthony Zarc uses as the backbone of his organization. That computer brain has a crass, malevolent sense of humor and tried to kill me with several metallic octopus arms. Only once though. The second time we met, he tried to capture me. And failed. Well, truth be told, Dermot gave me a helping hand that time. As far as I know, the only person who can give Hector orders is Anthony Zarc himself.

Hector had said I was outside his algorithms. I don't know exactly what that meant, but it made me feel special.

I hoped to stay outside his algorithms.

One of the men began talking again in Russian. It continued to mean nothing to me. Ten minutes of talk passed. Twenty.

I lay there, muscles tensed, ready to leap up at any moment. But nothing happened.

They were going to talk me to death. There was nothing more boring than a long conversation in another language. I yawned. I stretched a little, and my back made a cricking sound that I hoped no one heard.

Then one of the men said, "Amber Fang."

It was my name, clear as a bell, and the shock of hearing it ran up and down my spine. There was another long silence. I had this horrible sensation that they were all looking over the bar at me.

Then one of them laughed. And I became aware of their hearts and therefore realized their bodies were still in the same places. One heart was beating a bit faster, as though the mention of my name had made the owner slightly nervous.

Or angry.

It was the woman's heart. I knew that because it was smaller.

Then one of the men got up, made a sound that made me think he was stretching, walked directly to where I was lying, and, to my surprise, swung open a door to the "bar" that hid me. My legs must have blended into the carpet, because he stepped right over them. But I would be clearly visible if any of them at the table were looking.

I didn't dare move, because any motion would be easily spotted. So I stayed completely still.

He came back. I heard the ice crackle in the drink he was holding. He stepped over me and closed the door again. I had the overhang of the bar and my dark pants to thank for saving me.

I heard the man set down his glass on the table, and I sighed. That had been hellishly close!

Then the woman spoke up.

"A head shot has been okayed." She said this in English.

"A head shot?" one of the men asked. I'm not certain why they had switched to English.

"She can be brain dead, but not body dead," the woman explained.

Another shiver crept down my spine.

"So what would you use?" another man asked.

"Diamond-tipped shells." This was the woman's voice. And I had this horrible feeling I knew who she was. "They'll go through anything, but there's no mushrooming once they make contact, which will leave her brain dead but the rest of her still fully functional."

"You are that good of a shot?" This was a higher-pitched male voice.

"Yes," she answered. "Of course. You just have to hit her from the perfect angle."

Hit her? They were obviously talking about me. I didn't want to be accused of thinking the world revolved around me. But one way to keep my reproductive system in a peachy-keen condition was to put me in a coma. From a distance. Then Zarc could do whatever he wanted with my ovaries.

"Anthony's modules predict that the *Homo sapiens vampiris*'s brain matter will grow back," the woman continued. "In fact, he's tested the theory to limited success. And you get an easier-to-control subject. So it's the perfect solution."

We vampires do heal so much quicker than humans. Would our brains heal at the same rate? But what—or who—grows back into that gray matter? It looked like they had done some Mengele-like experiments. I wondered if they had been on my mother. No, not enough time had passed for her brain to grow back. And Anthony Zarc seemed to want to keep her healthy and in good condition.

Then again, Grigoriy had said Mom was *dead weight*. That her eggs weren't any good. Rendering her without value, as far as ZARC was concerned.

One of the others began talking in Russian.

"I recognize her voice, Amber," Dermot said.

"Yes, it's your ex-girlfriend," I subvocalized. "Hallgerdur Grettirsdottir." For some reason I felt it was important to say her full name. Maybe that would dispel her—send her back to Niflheim or whatever hell she'd crawled out of.

"You have to get out of there. Now!"

"I'll do my best. But I can't move yet."

They had returned to conversing in English again. Well, specifically, Hallgerdur had started to talk again.

"Those shells will go through anything," she said. "They'd even go through a wooden barrier on a bar." I swear her voice was now pointed in my direction.

I froze. I didn't want to move. I just pretended I didn't hear her words. But she *had* to be talking to me.

"Did you hear me, Amber?" she asked. There was that slight hint of Icelandic accent, but her English was otherwise perfect.

I could just pop up and say yes. But they would likely pop a diamond-tipped bullet through my head.

There was a *pffft* sound, and a hole appeared about two inches above me, spraying splinters across my back. My heart started flipping out—beating in overtime.

"The next one won't miss," Hallgerdur said. "Stand up slowly, Amber."

"Shit," I subvocalized.

"Get out of there!" Dermot screamed.

But that was not an easy option. In fact, there was no other option.

So I stood up slowly.

Hallgerdur was pointing a long-barreled pistol at me and smiling like she had just swallowed a tasty canary.

She looked the same as when I'd seen her in Iceland eight months earlier. Same blond hair. Same deadly figure (I mean that literally—she is nicely formed and viper-like). And those same iceberg-blue eyes.

And the same unwavering hand.

"Nice to see you, Hallgerdur," I said. "Read any good books lately?"

"The book of death," she said.

She raised the gun to point exactly at my forehead.

A TERMINATION

THERE ARE TIMES when seeing a familiar face can bring a glow to your heart. This was more of a burning pain. And the beginning of panic.

"How did you know I was here?" I asked, proud that I could keep my voice steady. "I am rather quiet."

Hallgerdur did that thing where the barrel of her gun doesn't waver an iota. It's distressing. I stole a quick glance at the four men. One was built like the Hulk but tanned brown and probably rented himself out as a bulldozer. The other three were somewhat nondescript. One was even wearing glasses, though I imagined they were just "cover" so he wouldn't stand out in a crowd. They had all drawn their handguns. The whole scene reeked of overkill.

I was just one eensy, teensy vampire.

"Hector told us you'd be here," said Hallgerdur.

That statement made me clench my teeth. The AI had predicted I'd be standing in a bowling alley in Sweden? I thought I was outside his algorithms. "How would he know?"

"Hector knows what he knows," she said.

Now Hallgerdur had turned into the Sphinx. But it did mean Hector had predicted I'd find Grigoriy in Belize and discover his ski hat and the card that would lead me here. What else was that devious artificial mind predicting?

"You're looking a little pale," Hallgerdur said. "I assume it's not just your complexion."

"Indigestion," I said, rubbing my tummy.

This caused her to give me a faint smile. "On that note, how is Grigoriy?"

"The cause of my indigestion," I said.

She somehow shrugged without allowing the bead on my forehead to waver. "Well, he knew the risks. I guess his little *I repent* gambit didn't work."

"It made him taste better," I said. "In fact, he tasted better than you." I hoped the dig would force her into some sort of mistake. But she only curled her lips up a little bit tighter.

I noted that one of the men—Bulldozer, I'll call him—narrowed his eyes and let out a little grunt of anger. My guess was that he knew Grigoriy personally. The others hadn't reacted.

Hallgerdur made a signal with her free hand, and Bulldozer went silent. But there was rage lurking behind his eyes. Now that was something I could perhaps build on.

He had known and liked Grigoriy. How to turn that to my advantage?

But I couldn't come up with a quick plan, so I said, "Your little computer commander can predict my actions. But how could he even know I would be in Belize?"

"There was more than one Grigoriy," Hallgerdur said.

It took me a moment to compute that. They had sent their killers—how many I couldn't guess—to beaches, to parks, all across the world. Then they had released their info into the wild and let me track them down.

Except I hadn't tracked him down. Agnes of the Returns had sent me a text with all the info. Maybe she'd come across it on a book search for *murderous assassins*.

Unless it wasn't her who had sent me the note. Unless someone else—Hector!—had written the text to make sure I was in Belize to meet Grigoriy. That thought was a little chilling. Perhaps my phone, the one I'd carried with me from Belize to Sweden, was being tracked too. They'd know all sorts of details. When I traveled. Where I stayed. Who I traveled with.

They'd also know my high score on Candy Crush.

"We are severely compromised," Dermot said in my ear. *Wow, no shit, Sherlock*, I wanted to shout back at him. I hoped they didn't know he was here. "Keep them talking though. I'll be there in a moment. Be prepared to plug your ears."

"Is that Dermot chattering at you?" Hallgerdur said. "I can tell by the way you bend your ear toward the earbud. Hello, Dermie! Hello! Can you hear this? Your girlfriend—"

"I'm not his girlfriend," I hissed.

"—will be incapacitated in a minute or two. But you, my dear, dear Dermie—you will be dead in just a few seconds."

"Ignore her," Dermot said. Then he made a weird grunt in my earphone. "What the hell is that?" he said. Something mechanical was talking in the background. "A clown. It's a damn clown. And—"

There was a click, then a buzzing and a thump, and at the same time came the loud, shattering percussion of an explosion. It rattled the doors of the bowling alley. A very big bomb had gone off across the street.

"Dermot?" I said. "Dermot. Answer me. Dermot!"

My earbud was dead.

"And thus ends the League." Hallgerdur made a faux sniff. "It is a grandly satisfying feeling to terminate my former employer and lover at the same time. Two birds with one explosive device. Though I'll miss Dermot's sad, disappointed eyes. He was especially sad and disappointed when I shot him."

Hallgerdur was very obviously wanting to get under my skin. And it was working, because that Fang anger was rising up from my guts, making me want to swing and scratch and bite. Damn the consequences.

"I am going to kill—"

"If you move, you're dead." Hallgerdur made a tiny circling motion with the gun. "This is how it will go from here, Amber Fang. You will put out your hands and be manacled. And we've brought along a dog muzzle—well, a vampire muzzle, really—to prevent bites. Then we'll package you up and travel to an unnamed and unknown destination. That's the best-case scenario. The other way for this to unfold is for you to make a sudden move and me to send a diamond-tipped bullet through your head. I prefer option two because we won't have to bother with the manacles or the niceties. We'll just package you up with Band-Aids on either side of your head. Please, please make a move."

I tensed my leg muscles. Began to crouch, but every micro-movement was followed by the slightest adjustment in her pistol. She couldn't miss from that distance. So I gradually straightened and took a deep breath.

I slowly raised my arms for the manacles.

Seven
CRY, BABY, CRY

BULLDOZER STEPPED AHEAD but approached from an angle, so that Hallgerdur still had a direct line to my forehead. He grabbed my hands and jerked them toward him with one meaty paw. His other hand pulled a large set of chromium manacles from his belt. I was certain they'd been tested against vampire strength. And once they were clicked closed, I'd have lost any chance to escape.

He clicked one over my left wrist so tightly that it pinched my skin. These manacles were not modern-day, sensitive-new-age-jailor approved! They were going to hurt. A lot. I could tell by the glare in Bulldozer's eyes that the second manacle would be even tighter.

I also spotted the curling of an octopus-tentacle tattoo that wrapped around his neck. It was a carbon copy of the one that had decorated Grigory. So this beefy gentleman was Russian too. Maybe he and Grigoriy had gone to the same tattoo parlor.

REVENGE

"Grigoriy tasted like vodka," I said. Bulldozer stiffened slightly and looked directly into my eyes. Yes, there was now a deep rage boiling inside him. I love making humans mad.

"You von't anger me," he said somewhat angrily.

"Was Grigoriy your friend? Your buddy? Or your lover?" A cheap shot, I know. I don't really care which human has sex with which other human—I only care which ones have sex with me. Oh, and how humans taste. The rest is none of my business. But I wanted to make him mad and thought a little homophobic slur might help.

"You. Vill. Not. Anger. Me," he repeated. But the muscles had bunched up along his neck. It was like watching a bull spotting a red cape.

Ugh! I couldn't think of any more clever taunts. *Thanks, brain!* This man was obviously tough and strong, and I wasn't certain I could outwrestle him. Of course, there was also Hallgerdur lurking behind him with her diamond-tipped death.

"Do your job, Alexei," she commanded.

Then inspiration struck. "He cried as he died," I said. "Wept like a little baby. Like a sissy girl. Like a ballet dancer in *The Nutcracker*. Like—"

Bulldozer slapped me. It was like being slapped by a giant holding a jumbo jet. My teeth rattled, my face burned, and my consciousness was almost knocked into next week.

But the slapping movement had brought him a half inch to his right, and he was now blocking Hallgerdur's line of fire.

He had also forgotten to click the second manacle in place.

Which left me free to punch him.

In the privates.

My fist bounced off. Ouch! Iron balls? No, he was wearing some sort of protection there. Damn, it hurt! But the blow angered him further, and he swung back to slap me again. Which gave me enough of an opening to set my feet and shove him hard.

There was a *pfft*, and a bullet shot through his left arm and perforated my lower shoulder. The wound was enough to sting and burn, but it didn't stop me—the bullet hadn't hit bone. Nothing could slow Bulldozer's momentum— he smacked into Hallgerdur, knocking her to the ground.

Which left a clear path for the others to shoot me. They brought up their guns.

I leaped up and smashed through the tiled roof. I was pleased to discover there was at least a foot of clearance. I scrambled left, then right, zipping along above the tiles, climbing upside down by clinging to the wooden ceiling. My enemies were shooting holes in the suspended tiles on either side of me. Dust and smoke filled my lungs, but I kept barreling along, working my way through the suspension wires and electrical wires and dust bunnies. Soon the shooting was farther behind me.

I paused to listen. I'd lost track of where I was. They had stopped shooting. Hallgerdur barked something in Russian, and I tried to slow my heart so I could hear their heartbeats or footsteps. But my ticker was racing madly.

I couldn't help picturing Dermot being blown to pieces. *Stop it! Stop it! Focus!* I told myself.

Then the tile behind me exploded in a spray of bullets, light shining through the newly formed holes.

The tile right in front of me, which I'd been thinking about crossing, became perforated. It was a game of tic-tac-toe-*die*. They were going to keep shooting until one of the tiles turned red. But did they want to flush me out? Or did they know exactly where I was?

And were they still concerned about keeping my insides intact?

The tile behind me erupted with holes. The smell of dust and gun smoke was enough to choke me now.

They knew I was here. I inched ahead to peer through a bullet hole. Hallgerdur was below me, standing on the pine floor of the bowling lane. She was eyeing the tile over to my left. There was a short burst of gunfire farther away. So maybe they didn't know where I was.

I sucked in a breath, tightened all my muscles and then shoved hard off the ceiling. I smashed through the tile, turning like a cat in midair so that I was directly facing my enemy. She began to raise her gun, but I knocked it from her hand and slipped my other arm around her neck. It was, I must say, the perfect move. A ten from the Russian judge!

Perfect, that is, until my feet hit the polished floor of the lane. Both of my traitorous clodhoppers shot up, and I thumped down hard on my derriere. Luckily, I brought Hallgerdur down with me. She tried to bash me with her head in order to get me to loosen my hold, but I used the gutter to push off, and, in a moment of grace, I was standing again with her head in a headlock. Bulldozer and two others were several feet away, pointing their pistols at me.

"Don't move or I'll break her neck," I shouted. Some spittle came out at the same time, which was a sign of me being a little frantic.

Hallgerdur had stopped struggling, but she turned her head enough to glare at me. She was either playing possum or had nowhere near my strength. Why would she need it? She was a sharpshooter. Extra muscle would be a waste.

One of the men said something guttural, and Hallgerdur hissed, "No."

I took a step behind me, dragging her along. And then another step, so we were now in the next lane and nearing the fire exit. I hoped the door wasn't blocked.

The mathematical part of my brain noted that there were only three men in front of me. The fourth was out of sight. That made me nervous. Maybe he was in the washroom, checking his phone

"I am going to enjoy when Anthony cuts into you to remove those vital parts," Hallgerdur said, her voice perfectly calm. "I will be there in the operating room. He listens to me. I will be certain you have no anesthetic. And I will, during every moment of your horrible pain, remind you of this moment." Her words were raspy, in part because I was squeezing her throat so tightly.

"That won't be happening," I said. "I'll die before you can cut me open."

"That can also be arranged," she said.

"If you want to live, you'll just move back with me, ever so slowly. I imagine those men are good shots. But I'm fast enough to use your head as a shield."

"I'll make a belt of your entrails," she said.

Ouch! She was getting primitive. What had Dermot ever seen in her? "No. For killing Dermot, if he is dead, I'll be wearing *your* entrails as a belt and your heart as a flower-decoration thingy."

Damn! I was sinking to her level. But without any eloquence. Why did Shakespearian insults flee my mind in moments like this?

"He was not the same anymore," she said. She almost sounded wistful. "He was tougher once. More interesting. The boring should die."

I kept squeezing her harder, and her breath grew ragged. "Don't say that! He was good. Good! He wasn't boring!"

I couldn't make out her next sentence. I had dragged her nearly to the exit door. I stepped onto the final lane.

A pair of hands shot out of the bowling pit, knocking aside the pins and grabbing my legs. The hands pulled hard enough to make me fall.

Eight
BOWLING A STRIKE

AS I FELL, I TWISTED MY ARMS. It was a move my *sifu* in Mexico City had taught me. It was not *wushu*, but a deadly tactic he'd learned on the streets.

Hallgerdur's neck made a cracking sound.

I hit the floor, let her roll away from me and tried to grab on to the gutter. The assassin who had hold of my legs was pulling me inside the pit with one hand while the other held a rather large eviscerating-type knife. He stabbed at me, and I jerked to the side. The blade stuck in the wood. I broke a bowling pin across his head, but it didn't slow him—his skull seemed to be made of stone. He stabbed again, this time hitting the meaty part of my left thigh. Pain shot through my leg. I gritted my teeth and desperately grabbed around beside me. His stabbing motion had brought him forward. I found a bowling ball with my other hand, slipped my fingers into the finger holes and swung it like a wrecking ball at his head.

It connected. Full force.

Can you say *rotten grapefruit*?

It was the grossest thing I'd seen since I accidentally kicked the head off a mobster. I nearly threw up, but instead I shoved his body away and glanced back.

Hallgerdur was lying still. Her neck lay at such a sharp angle that she was clearly dead.

I'd killed Dermot's ex-girlfriend. He was going to be so mad at me.

Then I remembered. He was likely dead. Or at least I couldn't be certain what the explosion had done to him.

Part of me didn't believe that someone as tough as Hallgerdur could be dead. But her heart had stopped beating—I couldn't hear it. And her chest wasn't rising. I was tempted to grab her feet and pull her over to be sure. Mom had always said it was permissible to kill in self-defense. So I wasn't feeling too much guilt.

Plus, Hallgerdur had shot Dermot. Twice.

The blood coming out of my leg was slowing, partly because pressure from the tactical suit was squeezing off the wound. But when I tried to move, it did squirt a bit, and the pain was nearly unbearable.

A noise drew my attention. Bulldozer was charging like a locomotive through the alleyway in the pit area. I knew if he got a hold of me, I'd be the train wreck.

I grabbed at the bowling-pin resetting machine to help me stand, slipped in the blood and gore, then got up again and stumbled toward the exit. Flight is the better side of valor, and there was no point in dying here.

Bulldozer moved faster than seemed possible for someone so bulky. He must have launched himself the last few feet, because he struck me right in the back, and we plowed into the exit door and skidded onto the street. The bright light blinded us both, but he recovered first, then grabbed the manacle swinging from my arm and clamped it onto the bar of the door handle. Then he swung a fist at my head, intending to pulverize it.

I ducked, and he punched a hole in the door. I hate to think what would have happened to my skull if he'd connected.

He punched again and I ducked again, and another fist-sized hole in the door duly appeared. I wasn't sure I could do this dance all day. Not with my leg the way it was. Besides, the other two agents would be arriving any moment. So I did something stupid.

But also brilliant.

I deflected his next punch, nearly breaking my right arm in the process. But his blow snapped the bar on the exit door. My manacle came free.

Then I set my good leg, grabbed the bar and snapped the rest of it off in one smooth move, and jabbed it into Bulldozer, knocking him over.

I fled.

In my best shape, I could have easily outdistanced him, but not today. I didn't dare look down at my leg. Despite the pain, I was able to find a bit of speed. Soon there were bullets flying, spraying bits of pavement at me. I stumble-raced past the building where Dermot and I had rented the apartment. The second floor—our floor—was a great big gaping hole that still belched smoke and flames. Dermot had been inside that mess. And there would have been no time for him to escape. Several Swedes were out on the street, still waiting for the authorities to arrive.

Adrenaline helped me push through the pain. Bulldozer was after me, even with the broken door handle sticking out of his side and his arm bloody from where Hallgerdur had shot him. He would put the Terminator to shame. The Swedes saw him and scattered like chickens. I didn't blame them.

But I had gained a bit of speed now, and I turned a corner, ran a few feet and quickly climbed a fire escape, grunting each time I used my left leg. I was out of sight on the rooftop before Bulldozer and the other agents could catch up.

I lay there, catching my breath, taking a tally of what parts of my body were still working. I could move my arm. Good. I could think. Good. My internal organs seemed to be functioning properly. The wounds were not superficial, but not so horrible that I'd die. They'd just slow me down. I tore off a piece of my tactical outfit and tied it around my thigh, effectively slowing the bleeding. With a few days' rest, I'd be good as new.

There was a whirring in my ears that I assumed was the rushing of my blood. Or just the adrenaline pounding through my system.

Then I squinted. A dark, dreadful shape appeared above me in the sky. A drone—a small one with four propellers and a camera. If it'd been armed, I'd be dead. But it was watching me.

I. Really. Hate. Drones.

Someone was coming up the ladder, and judging by the grunts and the shaking, it was Bulldozer. Likely whoever was piloting the drone was telling him exactly where I was.

I stood. Looked at the other rooftops. The farthest one, if I was in perfect shape, would be a long jump. But I didn't have much choice, so I ran toward it.

It dawned on me that the other assassins were likely climbing the fire escape in front of me, following the information the drone gave them. About the time I had that thought, a bullet whizzed by. I turned in midstride to present a smaller target. One of the assassins was at the top of the ladder ahead of me, his pistol flaring with each shot. I jumped, kicking the gun from his hand and smacking his head next, sending him down the fire escape.

I landed on the next roof, surprising myself. I was better than I thought!

The drone followed me as I dashed along the tiles. I'd never escape with those electronic eyes watching. I skidded to a stop, found a loose brick and threw it at the buzzing bundle of electronics. The drone zipped out of the way.

"Just my luck," I shouted. The person controlling it was an expert—I gave him the finger and thought I heard laughter come from the machine.

"Run, run as fast as you can, gingerbread Amber," it said. And I recognized Hector's annoying voice. "Don't trust the fox to help your plan—that'll be the end of the gingerbread woman!"

Great, not only was he trying to kill me, but he was also wrecking childhood songs.

There was more clanging on the fire escape behind me. One of the ZARC mercenaries took another shot, so I ducked behind a chimney, then ran, bent over, and leaped to the next building.

I almost made it. I banged into the wall, catching the very top bricks. Luckily, I could dig my nails in, and I still had enough arm strength to pull myself up, or I would have been a pancake.

This roof was slanted at a sharp angle, and with my bum leg I managed only a few steps before I tripped and started on a slide that would end with a three-story fall. I grabbed an antenna, probably wrecking some Swede's thousandth viewing of *The Girl with the Dragon Tattoo*. I crawled up to the chimney, using it to shield myself from the pistol fire of the mercenaries.

The drone hovered like an aggravating giant insect. "Best to surrender now, Buttercup," Hector said.

This time I grabbed three bricks. I popped up and aimed at the drone, throwing to the left and to the right. I aimed the third brick just below it.

I missed with the first. And the second. But the drone darted down to avoid both of them, and my third brick hit with a satisfying smack.

"I'll get you, my toothy friend! And your little mom too," Hector shouted as the drone spiraled down to crash into the concrete below.

I'd taken out their eyes. And punched Hector in the electronic nose.

But I'd also exposed myself to do that, and one of the mercenaries caught the edge of the chimney with a shot.

The bullet didn't hit me, but the shards of brick did, temporarily blinding me. I slipped and rolled down the roof, knowing I was about to take a very hard hit.

My eyesight cleared just as I reached the edge of the roof. I grabbed at the eavestrough and missed.

Then I fell.

Nine
THE GRAVITY OF THE SITUATION

THANK THE CITY OF UPPSALA for food recycling bins. It was a wheeled bin, and, fortuitously, a rare lazy Swede had left the lid up. I landed feet first in sludge and half-rotted foodstuff. The bin was deep enough and full enough to slow my fall and stop me from breaking my ankles. The leftover lefse and Swedish meatballs squirted and squished their way up the pant legs of my tactical outfit. The force of my impact made the bin roll down the street, and I became grimly aware that this whole scene likely looked comical from a distance.

I couldn't get out of the gunk. "Shit. Shit. Shit," I hissed. At any moment, one of my pursuers could race around the corner, and I'd be shot to death in a pile of disgusting food. Human food! An ignoble death for a vampire if there ever was one. The stuff was sucking me down like quicksand.

Then a sane, clear thought popped into my head. My struggling was making me sink. So instead of trying to kick and fight my way out, I just reached forward and grabbed the side of the bin and pulled, yanking myself out with a *thwurrrping*, burping sound. I threw my gunk-caked body over the edge, landed and tried to run. My feet slid, and I looked very Charlie Chaplinesque for a few seconds before enough of the crud and slime came off that I found traction.

I ran like a smelly wind, turning down a back alley. I cut left, then right, certain my friends wouldn't be far behind. After a block or so I stopped leaving footprints. I couldn't hear another drone. But the shot to my shoulder, the stab wound and general exhaustion were catching up with me.

Dermot and I hadn't cooked up an escape plan. We were walking on a wire with this operation, and there were no European safe houses for us to retreat to. I couldn't draw on whatever was left of the League—which might just be a few support staff. I didn't even have my passport.

All I had was a small, glowing sense of satisfaction.

I'd killed Hallgerdur. She'd seemed unstoppable the last time I met her. But she was dead.

This satisfaction didn't help my leg bleed any slower. Nor did it make me feel any better about Dermot. But the world was a shinier place without her in it.

I kept to the alleys, trying not to attract attention. I was not your typical tourist, and thankfully, the few Swedes who did see me didn't get in my way. Maybe a bleeding, smelly assassin was just normal for them. Or they were too polite to point out my appearance.

At one point I stumbled and lost my footing, smacking into a row of recycling and garbage stations. I'd read somewhere that the Swedes use their garbage for energy. I'd almost become a part of their system.

I saw three connected buildings across the street, with flags flying out front. The first section was a light reddish stucco, followed by a mostly glass structure, then finished off with a taller slate-gray building. There were at least a hundred bicycles out front. A big sign in the shape of a badge said *Polis*, and there was also a collection of white-and-blue cars with police lights on the top.

I could just duck inside the station, shout, "I'm an assassin from America!" and I'd be safe. Well, safe depending on how well armed the local police were—I assumed they didn't just round up criminals with hockey sticks and ski poles. But I would arrive with several suspicious wounds and no passport, so I'd be locked up in a cell in no time. And entered into their computer system.

I was pretty certain ZARC could crack their little Swedish codes and find me. So I limped past the police station, moving with as much speed as I could muster. I crossed a bike lane and four car lanes—what passed for a major thoroughfare in this city. Kitty-corner from the police station were a few trees that had grown up next to a small river. I leaned on each tree as I moved along, choosing not to take the bridge across the water. There were brick apartments on my left. I darted down an alley to avoid several joggers—they were certainly fit in this country. Everything was so damn clean—I wanted to apologize to each citizen I came across for all the blood and gunk and other stuff leaking off of me.

But instead I bled a bit more here and there and stumbled along. I was glad this wasn't the middle of rush hour. Even their downtown seemed extremely inactive. I did come close to passing out once or twice.

I stumbled around a corner and saw a word that made my heart glow.

Bibliotek.

The sign was at the top of a brick building with several rectangular windows. It was like seeing an oasis in the desert. In fact, I was so enthralled by the sight that I stepped out onto the street, and a small car narrowly missed me. Jeez, that'd be just my luck! Killed a few steps from safety. I bumbled along to the sidewalk, failed to stop properly and knocked over three bikes, which provoked consternation from several bystanders. They began to yell at me, but I didn't know the language, and it all started to sound like swearing. I threw my teetering body toward the side of the building, leaning on a green art installation for a moment. Then I climbed up the steps and made my way into a short passageway.

I was soon in an interior courtyard with a glassed-in roof and people reading books in what looked like an aquarium. Or a bookquarium. I tumbled through the first open doors I saw.

I was home! There was a library desk, and there were two librarians behind it. One male. One female. And I was a stinking, horrid mess, but I was also a bookworm. I wanted to hug them.

The female librarian said something to me in Swedish. She was clearly stressed at my condition.

"I am here for sanctuary," I said. I raised my hand in a sign of solidarity, making the handcuffs shake. "Tell the Returns. I claim sanctuary."

I sounded bat-poop crazy. But Theressa, the leader of the Returns, had once told me any library was safe. Or was that my imagination?

The woman said something soothing in Swedish, and her male co-worker started to come around the corner of the desk. He didn't look as calm as she did.

"Sanctuary," I said. "I want sanctuary. Do you know Theressa? My library card number is 121435. I'm friends with Agnes."

The man began making slightly aggressive Swedish-language noises and put his arms out as if he might grab me. He wasn't a large specimen. A lifetime of lifting books hadn't built his muscles.

"Does anyone speak English?" I shouted. My voice echoed in the library. Several patrons, who were watching me with a mix of confusion and pity on their faces, put up their hands.

"I do," a woman said.

"I do," an old man offered.

"I do," a mom with a stroller said.

Of course! People in Europe actually took the time to learn English. I was such a cultural boob sometimes.

"Any of the librarians?" I asked. "I need to talk to a librarian about sanctuary. I am one of you. I am one of you!"

A woman came out from behind a bookshelf. "Do you need help?" she asked in perfect English.

"My library card number is 121435 for the Université de Montréal and in the Seattle library it is 1023156. Though I am more than just a number!" I'm afraid I did sound like I was right on the edge of insanity.

"So you like libraries," the woman said. "That is good. Good. Many people like libraries. May I ask that you please keep your voice down. People are trying to read."

I guessed I'd been yelling. "I have come to talk to the Returns."

"The Returns?" the woman asked, with more than a little question in her voice. Perhaps just a hint of recognition.

"Yes, Theressa Dane is the metadata analyst. She's one of them. She is!"

"Please keep your voice down. My name is Sonya Svensson-Banerjee."

"Nice to meet you." I offered my dirty, messy hand, and she shook it without making a face. Her hand was warm. And clean. "Do you know Theressa? Or Agnes? I like Agnes. They're from the Preservational Librarians Guild." That seemed to light a lightbulb in her head. The male librarian had somehow moved closer behind me, and I spun, raising a hand and showing my claws, but I still had the presence of mind to leave my fangs unbared.

Sonya made a motion, and he backed away.

"Come with me, Amber," she said. She turned without looking back. So I followed her around a corner and past several rows of bookshelves. "You're safe here," she said over her shoulder. "Safe. You don't have to worry any further."

A part of me relaxed. I didn't realize how badly I needed to hear those words. She guided me through a set of glass doors and into an elevator. I leaned up against the side until I realized I was leaving a line of gunk on it.

"Oh, sorry," I said.

Sonya waved her hand. "It happens all the time. We get all types in the library, Amber. Some more interesting than others."

The elevator kept going down. Then the doors opened, and I followed her across a hall into what must have been her office. It had teak furniture and two chairs. The coffeepot was bubbling. With a quick motion, she closed all the blinds.

I stood in the center, my head full of wooze. I suddenly realized she'd spoken my name when we first met. And then again. But I hadn't told anyone my name.

How the hell could she know it? I opened my mouth to ask that exact question, but she put up her hand to silence me.

"I'm a Fanger," said Sonya. "It is such an honor to meet you, Amber Fang."

Ten
VISITING ELYSIUM

MY EYES WERE AS BIG AS OSTRICH EGGS.

"You can trust me," were the next words out of her mouth. "I am on your side."

I have to say, I relaxed. A Fanger! I imagined Sonya and my other fans getting excited every time I took out a book. Maybe they had their own "Let's Read What Amber is Reading" book club.

"Take a seat," she said. I went toward a chair covered in bright orange fabric, but she directed me to her leather desk chair.

"It's easier to clean," she explained somewhat apologetically.

Which is when I got a whiff of myself. It was horrid. I'm talking London-sewers horrid. Oh, matey! "I'm sorry," I said. "I seem to be both bleeding and stinking the place out."

"We all have our bad days," she said, as if I'd forgotten to comb my hair. She took my hand in her warm hands and deftly used a hairpin to unlock the handcuffs.

Umm, that's not a trick they teach in any Library Science master's class. But I didn't quite get my thoughts together enough to ask her where she'd picked up the skill.

She set the handcuffs on her desk. "Who is after you?"

"Assassins from ZARC. Men who are extremely well trained. But I took out their drone, so I don't think they could track me. I'm pretty sure I've lost them." I paused. "If I didn't lose them and they followed me here, do you ... well ... I mean, are you armed?"

She nodded. "We will handle it," she said.

I don't know why, but I got this image of an RPG launcher hidden in a cupboard under the front desk. More likely it was some sort of less lethal weapon that wouldn't damage the books or patrons.

"Sonic devices?" I asked.

She gave me a quizzical glance. "I'm not sure what you're asking, but just be assured you're safe. You can stop hyperventilating."

It took me a moment to realize she was right. I was mouth breathing heavily. I did my best to channel my qigong as I settled into the chair.

"Your English is perfect," I said.

"I studied in Texas," Sonya answered. "I seem to have lost my southern accent though, y'all." She didn't pause long enough for the joke to register. "Now let's get you cleaned up and stitched up." She lifted her smartphone and tapped a few buttons. "We're going to go down to the staff room where the showers are. I've had the hallways cleared of onlookers—you know how curious librarians can get. The fewer who know your actual identity, the better."

"That's kind of you." I was feeling quite a bit more lightheaded. I looked down at my leg and was pleased to see that not too much blood was leaking out. Though maybe the half-rotted food from the recycling bin had stuffed the wound. There was a horrible thought! The wound in my shoulder wasn't bleeding at all. "I—I had a partner. He was in the building across from the bowling alley."

"You were at a bowling alley?"

The way she said it made me wonder if I had been hallucinating the whole bowling experience. Then I remembered smacking that man with a bowling ball. It was an image I wouldn't dream up. "Yes, I was in a bowling alley called Latitude Dude. The apartment was on the second floor. It was destroyed. There was an explosion." Even as I explained the situation, it sounded hopeless. "He was ... he is a good man. I wonder ..."

"I'll send someone over right away. What's his name?"

"Dermot," I said. I didn't know if he'd want outside people to know his name, but too late for that. I told her the exact address of our Airbnb, and she sent a text on her phone. "It's handled. We'll find out everything possible."

Then Sonya helped me out of the chair and, putting an arm under my good shoulder, guided me into the elevator and closed the doors. It went down. She smelled fresh and pine scented. "Can—can you contact the Returns?"

"They are not meant to be contacted. They just appear."

The way she said it made me wonder if she was one.

"That's not very helpful."

"No. It isn't in this case. But I will send a message to the powers that be," she promised.

We were soon in a staff room, and off to one side was a large washroom with concrete shower stalls. "Are you able to bathe yourself?" she asked.

"Yes. Yes." I waved her away and closed the door. Then, using the wall to hold myself up, I made my way to the shower stall. I stripped out of my suit and examined the bullet wound in my lower shoulder. I was surprised at how little damage there was. Yes, the bullet had torn flesh, but most bullets are designed to mushroom out and make a big mess. This one had gone right through me, catching the top part of my pectoral muscles (and missing bone, thankfully). I remembered Hallgerdur talking about the diamond-tipped bullets meant to lobotomize me. My guess was, all those mercenaries had been packing them. Maybe that was why I still had a functioning shoulder. Timing was on my side too—one of the side effects of being wounded close to a feeding day is that I tend to heal faster. That was something I'd noticed even in my teen years.

I cranked on the water, let it get nice and hot, then shoved myself under the spray. Soon my hair was wet, my muscles relaxing as the blood and garbage sluiced off me. Using the soap felt like a holy ritual. A shampoo called Såklart was heavenly. I eventually felt like a vampire again. A clean one.

Then I just leaned against the stall and let the heat sink into my muscles. I couldn't help but think of Dermot. I pictured his face and that somewhat chiseled jaw. He had a gentle manner, yet a hard interior when needed. Could he really be gone?

Logic told me he was dead. There hadn't been time for him to escape such a devastating blast. He *was* gone. He had to be. Those eyes. All of him. Gone.

I shed tears freely. The shower washed them away. The last time I'd wept that hard was a few days after Mom first vanished.

A knock on the door made me sniff in surprise. "Are you okay in there?" Sonya asked.

"Y-yes," I said, surprised at how weak my voice sounded. "Yes. I'm fine. Fine. I'll be out in a moment."

I turned off the water, found a long white towel and wrapped myself in it. When I stepped out of the bathroom, Sonya was standing there with a fresh change of clothes. "Several of my coworkers volunteered to help dress you— I mean, give you clothes to dress in. They're all clean." There was a pair of jeans, a tank top, a gaudy, bright-green sweater, underwear and socks. Even a pair of running shoes.

"That many of you know who I am?"

She shrugged. "What can I say? Word got around. And so many of us are Fangers. We don't want to be Fangers-on though."

She laughed at her own pun and then turned away as I put on the underwear and tank top. When I was done she helped me bandage the bullet wound, which was now leaking a bit. She also dressed my leg. She didn't flinch once. "Finally I get to use my first aid," she said. I looked at her curiously. "We saw a lot of bullet wounds in Texas," she explained.

"Really?" I said.

"No. I'm playing to the stereotype. But it was one of the scenarios we practiced. So I am pleased that I finally get to apply what I learned."

In short order I was patched up and dressed. Sonya even handed me a hairbrush. Soon I looked almost like it had been just another day—no one would guess the crap ride I'd been on.

There was a knock on the staff-room door. "Enter," Sonya said, and the librarian I'd seen at the front door came in. He had a yellow racing-bike helmet on and was sweating. "What did you discover?" she asked him.

He looked at me and back at her. "They were taking bodies out. In bags," he said. So he did speak English. "There were several police cars and ambulances. There was very little left of the apartment. If your friend was in there, then he..." He trailed off.

"Did you see who was in the body bags?" I asked.

He shook his head. "Zipped up," he said.

"Thank you, Matts," Sonya said.

He gave me one more glance and looked like he was about to say something comforting, then turned away and left the room. I, of course, had hoped the news would be different. But Dermot had to be dead. I gritted my teeth.

Sonya patted my back. "If you want, I can contact hospitals. And...and morgues."

"No. I just need access to a computer terminal."

"We have one down here."

She led me to a laptop in the corner of the kitchen. I clicked around, then said, "Is there an easy way to visit the dark web?"

"Oh, yes, let me show you." Sonya reached over and typed in a few numbers and letters. The Tor browser popped up, and I dived into the dark web. I went to a room that Dermot had created. He'd called it Elysium as some sort of clever reference to Greek mythology. The place where heroes go when they die—it didn't sound so funny now. I clicked somewhat desperately on several documents and then found the chat room. There were no messages. He hadn't tried to reach out.

He had to be dead.

"I have to get out of Sweden," I said.

Sonya nodded. "That can be arranged." Just then her phone buzzed. "We have had a message from the Returns. It reads: *We cannot help AF further at this time. Our policy of noninterference disallows that. You have fulfilled your duties by bringing her back to health. You will follow the catch-and-release protocol.*" Sonya didn't read the message with any gusto.

"They are rather rigid about their policies," I said.

"We librarians do love our policies."

"Yes. And I suppose I understand. Libraries and librarians aren't supposed to take sides."

"No, we aren't," Sonya said. "But that doesn't mean we can't point you in the right direction."

She handed me a leather passport. It was Canadian, and it had my photo in it.

"How did you put this together?"

"Let's just say the Fangers have a few pictures of you. And my many classes in binding and copying have not gone to waste. I threw this together while you were showering."

It was a perfect document. And she'd chosen the name Alice Cullen.

"You named me after a vampire in *Twilight*!" I nearly spat the words.

"Yes, I thought it was funny. It's one of my favorite books." My estimation of her was dropping by the moment. "A guilty pleasure," she added, perhaps seeing the tinge of distaste on my face.

I was being stupid. Just because I looked down on a book didn't mean another reader wouldn't be able to find joy and maybe depth in it—or at least escape. Librarians are not supposed to be judgmental. "It's a very clever choice,"

I said without sarcasm. "Though next time, a nonfictional, nonrecognizable name might be better."

"I should have thought of that." She tapped her forehead. "Forgive me."

"I'll proudly carry it. Maybe being named after a vampire will bring good luck."

I felt in the pockets of my sweater—there was nothing in them because, of course, only minutes before, these clothes had belonged to someone else. "Ah, this may seem like an over-the-top request, but do you happen to have a phone that is unlocked and untraceable? I realize the chances are slim. It's just that it's hard to—"

She put up her hand. "Here is my *pièce de résistance*," she said. "I had a feeling you'd need to communicate." She brought a black phone out, and my eyes grew wide. It was an ancient Blackberry—well, at least two years old. She was also holding a set of black wireless earbuds.

"I didn't think anyone used a Blackberry anymore."

"Oh, you'll find this baby is one of a kind."

She acted like she was handing me Excalibur. I was surprised when I tapped the screen and a female voice said, "Hello, Amber."

"Uh, hello," I answered.

"I look forward to being at your service. I await your commands," the phone said.

"Uh, is it AI?" I whispered.

"Not quite full AI, but you'll find the phone very intuitive. It has our secret operating system on it: Athena."

"The Greek goddess of wisdom. Good choice."

"She's also the goddess of planning," Sonya said, beginning to librarian-splain mythology. "And war. Our war is against lack of knowledge."

"I'm with you there, sister." There was a little keyboard at the bottom of the phone—old-fashioned tech melded to new tech. I liked that. "It looks great."

"Thank you," Athena said. "The black is slimming, right?"

I stared at the phone and laughed. "Well, she's really something! And the phone is untraceable, I assume, and unhackable?"

"Neither the CIA nor the NSA could crack our ice." Her voice reverberated with pride. "Or Anonymous, for that matter."

The CIA wasn't known for having the best coders on the planet. Perhaps too much testosterone there to code properly. "I look forward to discovering its—uh, her—capabilities." I put the phone in my pocket. "But I do have to get out of Dodge, so to speak."

"I'll give you a ride to the airport. It's in Stockholm, south of us."

One elevator ride and a short walk down the street later, I was sitting in her car. It was electric—which didn't surprise me at all. Being freshly washed and freshly dressed, I felt almost like I was a normal citizen going on a ride with a friend.

Except for my aching wounds.

The ride to the airport took around an hour. With the heat cranked up in the car, I soon fell asleep—blame it on complete exhaustion. When I opened my eyes again, Sonya was pulling up to the passenger departure area of Bromma Airport.

She got out of the car and put out her hand to shake mine. To my complete surprise, I hugged her. *I'm becoming a softie!*

"Good luck, Amber Fang," Sonya said. "From me and all the Fangers."

Eleven
CONTACT MADE

THANKFULLY, I WAS EASILY ABLE TO PURCHASE a ticket by accessing funds my mother had left in an account several years ago. I went into the airport, feeling like my lime-green sweater and jeans were the perfect cover—none of my enemies would expect me to be dressed like a middle-aged librarian. The floors inside the airport were so clean they almost glistened, the sunlight coming in from a line of windows near the ceiling of the building. There were not that many people around, which I preferred—though sometimes it was easier to hide in a crowd. Either it was a slow time or it never got busy at this airport. I had no idea where Swedes would be traveling to. Disneyland? The Bahamas? The North Pole? I don't have very many Swedish stereotypes, just that they are extraordinarily healthy. That's a bit hard to joke about.

I found a cushioned chair to sit on and gathered a few of my thoughts. I hadn't quite awakened from the nap. I decided it was best not to catalog my aches, especially not the one in my heart.

But ZARC now had full knowledge that I was in Sweden, so I had to get out of here. Even sitting in the airport made me feel like a target. I looked around for security cameras and spotted several along the ceiling. Could Hector hack into them? Maybe. I had no idea what the limits of his abilities were. And there was nothing I could do to prevent it.

Well, a flight was the quickest way out of Sweden. A boat or train would take too long. I just had to hope I was far enough ahead of my enemies.

I took out my phone and Athena showed me the time and the weather. I didn't know where to go next, but I knew I had to choose somewhere unexpected. I thought about Iceland—going to Hallgerdur's home country would perhaps be outside of Hector's algorithms. But it's a small country, population-wise, and quite homogenous, so that meant I'd be much easier to track. A trip back to the States would be just the ticket, except being in a plane for so many hours made me nervous. That would give them time to track me down and capture me once I landed. I just had to get out of here quickly, yet not spend too much time in the air.

Actually, what I wanted to do was find a cab and tour every morgue to be sure Dermot was dead. I needed to see his body, and I shivered at the thought of him lying on a cold table, alone. I got an even worse chill when I imagined ZARC finding him, taking a snapshot of his dead body and marking him off their kill list. Or they might even steal his body for some nefarious purpose. But hanging around hospitals and morgues, which were most likely watched by ZARC agents, was not a wise idea.

I tapped my way back to the dark web, surprised at the speed of the operating system on the phone—not even a microsecond of delay. But Dermot hadn't left any messages at Elysium. Then I cast about for places to visit and drew several blanks. Finally I settled on roulette. I slipped in one of the earbuds, lifted the phone and whispered to Athena, "Choose a country for me to fly to."

"I hear this city is beautiful this time of year," she said.

A night image of an exquisite parliament building on the Danube appeared. It was lit up with lights, a marvelous city spread out behind it: Budapest.

It was perfect. A large city. A massive tourist influx. It would be so easy to hide there. Plus, I'd never been there. There would be a high contingent of English speakers because of the tourism. The more I thought about it, the more I wanted to thank Athena.

So I did. "Thanks," I whispered.

"Anytime, Amber," she said. "I'm here to support you."

Just hearing that made me feel safer. Athena was amazing! And gee, was I already anthropomorphizing an operating system on my phone? I'd soon be one of those lonely people talking to Siri by candlelight on Friday nights.

I booked a Brussels Airlines flight that had one stop before landing in Budapest. Then I downloaded my ticket and went through security. They apparently weren't *Twilight* fans, because no one questioned my new name. I didn't have a book with me, having left *Life of Pi* on the beach in Cuba, so I slept and awoke only as we were descending toward the city.

The Budapest airport was jam-packed with tourists. My heart soared at the sight. I mean, I hated being so close to that many humans, but it would be so much easier to blend into the crowd. I always kept a hand near my face or looked down, in case the security cameras had some sort of facial-recognition system

I zipped through the airport—having no suitcase to pick up made that easy—and threw myself into the nearest shiny yellow taxi. "Take me to a medium-sized, run-of-the-mill hotel," I said.

The driver nodded, and soon enough we were in the heart of Budapest. He stopped before an art nouveau hotel called the Liechtenstein Apartments. It was an old building, several stories high, and it looked like it might be a bit more expensive than I'd intended, but I could afford it. I paid the driver in euros and got out, looking up at my new home. I honestly had no idea which quarter of the city I was in. And perhaps if I didn't know, then ZARC wouldn't be able to find me.

Within a few minutes I was in my room on the fifth floor. I threw myself down on the bed, stretching out on top of the red comforter. I'd check my wounds later. At least they hadn't bled through any of my clothing—Sonya had obviously been paying attention in first-aid class. I succumbed to that horrible habit so many humans have—I looked at my phone before going to sleep. The first place I went to was Elysium.

There was a message waiting for me in the chat room. It was titled *Urgent*. My heart started to beat faster. "Dermot! Dermot! You bastard, you're alive!"

I tapped on the message.

Hello, Amber, it's me, Agnes.

That's all it said. But there was a little chat box below it with a flashing cursor that waited for my reply. My heart sank like a submarine on fire. It took me several moments to work up the energy to chat back.

Agnes? How did you find Elysium?

I watched the cursor for a minute. Five minutes. Ten.

I nearly threw the phone across the room, but worried that it might somehow hurt Athena. Anthropomorphism again!

Then these words appeared: **Found your Elysium room through an intermediary.** What the hell did that mean? **I have discovered your mother. I know where she is. She is not safe.**

Agnes had covertly slipped me the location of my mother the last time I met her. Perhaps uniting me with my mother was an obsession of hers. Those Fangers would do anything for me.

Is this really you, Agnes? I honestly had no idea who to trust. ***Where did we meet?***

In books. The answer came back immediately. But what did it mean? We hadn't met in books. She'd first seen me in a warehouse in Oxford and helped get me into a bookmobile that took us to Bromley House Library in Nottingham. So was she just being coy by saying books?

What do you mean?

We know each other through books. Books. Libraries. Sorry, the keys are not working. It's an old phone. But books. Moving books.

A bookmobile?

Yes. You remember that. I don't have much time. They'll find me. And I'll be imprisoned again. Maybe killed.

Killed?

Yes, ZARC has me. I broke out of my room. But can't escape this compound.

What? What would they want with a librarian? Even a ninja librarian.

We reached out to them. Bad move. Several librarians dead. They killed them. Killed them. Captured me.

I could only imagine her crying as she typed this.

Where are you?

I am...

The chat came up with that *dot dot dot* that meant someone was typing. I stared at the *dot dot dot* until I thought I'd go mad. Then I set the phone down.

I picked it up a second later.

Where? I texted again. ***Where!***

Neuschwan Eagles. East woods. CH. They are coming. Your mother in danger here. Oh, I must run.

Then the chat box closed and disappeared. It was as if someone had wiped the whole conversation from the dark web's memory. Actually, perhaps the whole point of the dark web is that it has no memory.

I clicked my way out of Elysium and immediately went back in. No new messages.

Neuschwan Eagles. East woods. CH. That's what she'd written.

Great. I had a fragment poem to use to hunt down my mother. To find Agnes and ZARC.

I lay my head back on the pillow. Agnes was in danger or at least felt she was. And she could be anywhere in the world. There was nothing I could do to help her right now. Even if I knew her exact location, I couldn't get there fast enough to rescue her. I'd just have to hope she was exaggerating the threat.

And, I also knew, I'd reached the end of my reserves. My mother had always told me, *You think like crap when you're overtired.* She was right. A few hours of sleep would help me heal and get my brain back into proper thinking mode. I'd be able to solve my problems much faster than if I threw myself at them in this exhausted state.

I lay back and said, "Please set yourself to *do not disturb*, Athena."

"I will, Amber," she said. "Also, I have chosen a song for you. Have a lovely rest."

She began to softly play Johannes Brahms's "Lullaby."

To my surprise, I fell asleep.

Twelve
WONDERFUL WORLD OF

BUDAPEST IS LOVELY IN JUNE. The city's main attraction is the Hungarian Parliament Building, which is Gothic Revival to the core, with a massive dome in the middle, spires and parliament halls on either side. It puts all other parliaments to shame. There are impressive bridges across the Danube, the river the Vikings loved so much and the Romans used to mark the boundaries of their empire. In fact, there are ancient Roman bath houses in the city that turn into discotheques at night. I discovered this when I walked by one that was in the open, full of people in bathing suits splashing around and dancing as if they were in a nightclub. The city is brimming with history.

I had awakened at dark and walked the streets of Budapest. I felt safer then. No people or facial scanners were likely to recognize my face. And though it was just a bit after midnight, the city was vibrant with nightlife. The air was still warm enough to make me sweat a little as I walked. I find that my brain always works better while I am taking a stroll.

I had the slightest limp from my leg wound, but I did my best to disguise it. Predators note weaknesses and soon circle in for the kill. I know all about that.

There were swarms of crowds, and oddly enough, most of them were going in and out of museums. The reason for this became clear when I overheard a British tourist in gaudy khaki shorts declare, "There is nothing more refreshing than the bracing joy of the night of the museums." What that meant was that every museum in Budapest is open until 2:00 AM.

"Insanity," I whispered. But my librarian heart thrilled at the idea and ideals behind these kinds of events. Public art for the masses. Who cared if some drunk vomited at the foot of Venus de Milo? At least they were looking at art.

I skipped the Museum of Terror, which documents the victims of Nazi and Communist regimes. Important, but I needed something a bit more uplifting. The Hungarian National Gallery is an impressive building with Roman columns, a dome (they like their domes here!) and more paintings than you can shake a paintbrush at.

But once I was inside, the crowds were thicker and—well, I do have a sensitive nose—smellier. Seeing such a wonderful display of paintings made me think of the underground bunker I'd visited in Antarctica and all the paintings that had been destroyed when Hector blew the building to kingdom come. That reminded me of how I'd rescued my sister, Patty, from that compound. It had been the place I'd discovered I had a sister—a branch of the family tree my mother had neglected to tell me about. My dear psychotic sister wasn't so much interested in sister bonding—she was eagerly interested in yanking out my ovaries and the rest of my reproductive system and using them to get vampires back into the fertility game.

But could I use my ovaries against them? I wondered if there was a way to fool my vampiric brethren into invading ZARC, creating enough of a distraction that I could rescue Mom. That is, if I could discover ZARC's base from the crappy hints I'd been given.

I thought about it. And thought about it. If I were Napoleon or Queen Zenobia, I'm sure a plan would have popped fully formed into my brain.

Too many intangibles. Getting other vampires involved was like inviting vipers to an already crammed snake pit. Besides, I couldn't make any plans until I knew where ZARC and my mother were.

A man cleared his throat next to me—in an aggravating manner. Apparently, I was staring too long at the painting *Lady in Violet* by Pál Szinyei Merse. I gave the patron my *I'll tear your throat out before I move from this spot* look. He quickly glanced down and shuffled around me.

There was a commotion at the far end of the room, but far too many people were in the way for me to spot the source. A man yelled in English, "Hey, he's got my phone!" Then someone screamed—a high-pitched horror-film scream. "He pinched me!" Several people laughed. I glimpsed a man in black race down a stairwell at full speed, followed by two other smaller men, also in black. Then the crowd closed in, and it all calmed down. But the whole scene made me nervous. I don't like unexplained events.

Obviously, the artwork wasn't calming me down.

I suddenly felt surrounded by the crowds—a sardine in a tin can of culture. So I pushed and pulled my way out of the influx of art goers, burst outside and took a few deep breaths the moment I was several steps away from the building. I wandered for a bit, catching my breath, wishing I had Dermot to complain to.

Just thinking of him made my heart hurt.

Even walking was becoming too much for me. So I found an outdoor café, sat at a table and ordered a tall dark coffee. I soon discovered that they know how to do coffee in Hungary. I assumed that had something to do with their winters. Or maybe they are just that much more classy than us Americans. The Europeans generally do seem to understand coffee better than we do. Perhaps it is steeped in their culture.

I could almost forgive myself for using that pun.

Anyway, the back burner of my brain was still percolating with questions, like *How will I find ZARC? Or Mom? Or Agnes?* But it was becoming clear that I couldn't solve the puzzles just by throwing my brain directly at them.

So with coffee in hand, humanity swirling around me, I took my phone out.

First, I went to Elysium and discovered there were no new messages. Which was a double disappointment. I still expected a message from Dermot—well, I had to have hope, right? But there was no way I could imagine him surviving an explosion that had taken out the whole floor. Yet...those people who lost their family members on flight MH 370 still believe, impossibly, that their loved ones are alive. There is something very human about that.

I had to remind myself that I'm not human.

To take my mind off those thoughts, I recalled the little fragment of hints Agnes had given me.

Neuschwan Eagles. East woods. CH.

It had to be a location. But where the hell were the East Woods? Or the Eagle East Woods. And the first word—if I was even spelling it correctly—looked German. Or Bavarian. And finally, what could *CH* stand for?

So I did what any secret assassin would do when confronted with a problem like that. I googled it.

There are a lot of junior baseball teams with the name East Woods Eagles. There's also Mrs. Eastwood's fifth-grade class, whom she called "the eagles of science." Cute! But not helpful. So no leads there. I did get the feeling that I was missing an important clue.

"More coffee?" asked my male server. He was in his twenties with a thin, tanned face. I didn't look at his neck because

I wasn't hungry. I nodded, and he filled my cup, then said, "There is so much to see. So much life here."

He motioned toward the open square, where a multitude of humans were interacting—living, breathing, laughing. And here I was, staring at my phone. His tone hadn't sounded judgmental.

"There is," I said. "So much life. Thank you."

I would look around at Budapest once I'd solved this little puzzle.

I entered the word *Neuschwan*. And Google immediately regurgitated the words *Schloss Neuschwanstein*. Or, as further reading showed me, *Castle Neuschwanstein*. It was a white, many-spired castle on a rugged, green hill in Bavaria, Germany. It looked so familiar to me, but I couldn't recall reading about it. I guessed I'd spent too much time dreaming about living in Dracula's castle. The familiarity hit home when I read that this castle had been the basis for the palace in the opening of every Disney movie and TV show.

I'm a sucker for Disney movies. It's a weakness. I even like their version of *The Hunchback of Notre Dame*.

Castle Neuschwanstein is an impressive piece of nineteenth-century architecture, built by Ludwig II, king of Bavaria—who was also known as Mad King Ludwig. He had to be insane to spend so much on a castle long after the Middle Ages were over.

But there was something romantic about that. An idealist. Trying to hold on to the past.

I love idealists. Their blood tastes more innocent.

That's actually one of Mom's jokes.

I continued to search images of the castle. It was incredibly impressive, even in photographs. But there was no way ZARC was in Castle Neuschwanstein. Over fifty million people have walked through the castle since it was opened to the public. You can't hide a multinational arms-dealing organization in the wide open like that.

Neuschwan Eagles. East woods. CH.

And my frog brain, being a jumpy, untrustworthy creature, got stuck on Mrs. Eastwood's class, and I couldn't get past it until I remembered something. Clint Eastwood. I was reminded that my mother had forced me to watch every one of his movies. Over and over and over again. Clint was handsome, of course, but I didn't totally understand her obsession. Was it because he played violent characters yet in real life was a vegan? Did she like that contradiction? Eastwood. Eagles.

Eastwood. Eagles.

I felt like I had something there. Almost just on the edge of my knowledge. Of intuition.

Nah. Nothing.

Then *Where Eagles Dare*. It was an Eastwood movie set in World War II, and it involved the rescue of a general captured by the Germans in a castle in the mountains. The movie was Mom's favorite and, I admit, a good one. She'd wear Clint's undershirt while she watched it.

There must be a castle that looked like Castle Neuschwanstein hidden in the mountains. His movie had been filmed somewhere in Germany. Maybe this "similar" castle was hiding there.

I was onto something. I was certain of it. I was getting much closer to figuring out the location of Agnes and ZARC and my mother.

And maybe I'd be able to get my vengeance. Let me make a list: Hector and Anthony Zarc. The top of my kill list.

I looked at the letters *CH*. The last of the words Agnes had texted to me. Of all the clues, it fit the least. Again, nothing would pop into my head, so I slipped in my earbud and whispered, "Athena, google *CH*."

It always felt like cheating when I googled, but this wasn't a crossword puzzle.

"Okay, Amber. Here's what I found," Athena whispered back.

A list appeared on the phone's screen.

Methylidyne—something to do with chemistry. Not helpful.

Cluster Headache. Well, that was what I was feeling at the moment.

Cargo Helicopter. Ugh!

Then, finally, *Confoederatio Helvetica*.

It is the Latin name for Swiss Confederation, or Switzerland, as the Swiss like it to be called. And Switzerland has mountains and ski hills and maybe enough space to hide a ZARC compound.

Could it be that easy?

I leaned back and sipped my coffee. These European countries were small, but it wasn't like I was going to find the hidden palace just by catching a bus to the Alps.

So I dropped down the rabbit hole of the dark web and searched my keywords there. There's a lot of garbage on the dark web, and more Bitcoin sales of meth than you can shake a needle at. But after about twenty minutes of searching I discovered a small page put up by an off-piste (or "out-of-area") skier, who said his friend Fat Bones Franklin had disappeared in the Swiss Alps near an alpine train station with the itchy name of Grütschalp. Fat Bones had been searching for the perfect powdered snow in the backcountry. Most people assumed he had died in an avalanche. But the last text from Fat Bones was reported to be **I found Castle Neuschwanstein!** A very strange text, since he wasn't in Bavaria. The blog mentioned his exact geotagged location. No one had ever found his body.

Or explained his nickname. Some kind of ski-bum joke, I imagined.

Fat Bones vanished last year. Two others had disappeared the year before that in the same area.

Bingo. This had to be where ZARC was hiding.

Plus, it was all I had to go on.

I finished off my coffee, getting my last hit of caffeine.

Then I marched toward my hotel.

Thirteen
A PECULIAR SNIFFING

I WAS WIRED when I returned to my room. The coffee was rocketing through my bloodstream. And I was flushed with the energy I get from being around so many humans—it's such a dichotomy. Part of me loathes them. Another part of me comes to life being in crowds. It is the same feeling as being at a concert—I can put up with the crush (and the smell) just to get that energy. To be a part of something bigger.

But I was alone in my room, and I wanted to bounce off the walls. I checked Elysium for the thousandth time, and there were no new messages. Obviously, I couldn't take a flight in the middle of the night. But first thing in the morning, I would make my way back to the airport, become Alice Cullen again and wing my way west to Zurich.

I didn't get under the covers, but I lay down on the bed, not even taking the time to remove my shoes. I closed my eyes, intending to nap. Sleep did not arrive. I was somehow bone-tired and keyed up. I listed the wounds I'd received since meeting Dermot and lost count. Not that I could blame it all on him. But I had been darted, shot, poked in the nose, shot again and generally put through the wringer. But no broken bones.

I wanted to laugh with him about each bruise. We could exchange war stories.

But the bastard was gone. I hugged a pillow, then placed another between my knees, a comforting habit I'd developed in childhood.

There was a sound outside my door, just the creak of floorboards, and I became aware of four hearts beating in the hallway. Three large hearts and one smaller—a female one—and I thought of Hallgerdur. But she had to be dead.

I was pretty sure of that.

Then there came a sound that, to be honest, was very odd.

Sniffing. Like someone was sniffing around the door. It was the same sound you'd hear in a bathroom if a man were nasally testing the effectiveness of his armpit deodorant on a date night.

I slid carefully out of bed and crept up to the door, bracing for it to burst open at any moment. Somehow ZARC had found me. I leaned forward and looked through the spy hole.

It was dark. Black. Either broken or...

Someone had put their finger over it.

"Are you certain this is her room?" a male voice said. It was so guttural and raspy it creeped me out. It sounded like the man had smoked a tractor trailer full of cigarettes.

"Yesssss, Massster, it is," another man replied. But the tone of voice suggested he was putting on an affectation. One male heart sped up. The other hearts didn't. I didn't know what that meant. "I can smell the bitch from here, sssssir." Someone—the speaker, I figured—scratched his fingers along the wall. "Oh, in fact, she'ssss on the other side of the door. Right now."

Crap!

Something banged hard against the door.

I jumped back, looked around for a weapon and then realized I didn't want to be cornered in the room. They'd have guns. Darts. Or diamond-tipped bullets. Taking on four of them at once in such close quarters was not wise, especially since they were already prepared. Who could say what tools they had with them? For all I knew, they could slip a bomb the size of a piece of paper under the door. I leaped over the bed, tore apart the gauzy, gaudy yellow curtains and grabbed the window, yanking it upward. It shattered when it hit the top, and at the same time one of the men yelled and hit the door even harder. It popped open, but the chain held.

I climbed onto the sill, kicking the glass out of the way. I was glad I hadn't taken my shoes off. There was an overhang, and a precarious eavestrough that may have been around since the '50s. I grabbed on and clawed my way to the rooftop. Then, for some reason, I took a second to lean over and look down toward my room.

Someone stuck their head out of the window—they had a balaclava on. The person looked left, then right, then turned and stared directly up at me. A heartbeat later a crossbow was pointed in my direction.

Which is when I ran.

The hotel was taller than the next building, so I dashed a bit of a distance and jumped across an alleyway. I hoped, of course, that I wouldn't tear my wounds open again. But I landed adroitly and kept running, jumped another alleyway, then ran and jumped again, all the while listening for drones. I didn't hear one. Maybe they hadn't had time to get one up in the sky. I scrambled down a wall onto a cobblestone street. There were still so many people out, even though the museums would be closed by now. I burst through the clumps of humans, trying to find safety, then slowed and made sure I blended in with the crowds.

A minute later I spotted a vacant cab going by and waved at the driver like a maniac. Before he'd even properly stopped, I was in the back seat and tossing a handful of euros his way. "To the airport," I huffed. "I'm in a hurry."

My driver was female, which made me feel safer. She smiled a racer's smile and hit the gas. I couldn't help glancing over my shoulder to be sure we weren't being followed. There was no one else on the street. I had no idea how ZARC had found me. I'd left no trail that I was aware of. I'd trusted Sonya when she said the phone was untraceable. And I was pretty certain there was nothing implanted in my body.

And, to top it all off, one of them had been sniffing outside my door. Sniffing! Like they were scenting me out.

And he'd called the other "master." It sounded like an odd relationship. That was not how mercenaries usually spoke to each other.

In a relatively short time we arrived at the airport. I tossed a few more euros to the driver, who flashed another grin, and got out of the cab. I was still in the same clothes I'd been wearing when I arrived. I hadn't even had time to pick up a backpack.

Well, that meant I wouldn't have to worry about carry-on luggage.

Within an hour I, and by that I mean Alice Cullen, was on a plane to Zurich.

Fourteen
ITCHING THE GRÜTSCHALP

I RENTED A CAR IN ZURICH.

I'm a horrible driver. Mom, when she was around, did all of the driving. I was so fleet of foot that I'd tended to walk or, because we lived in larger cities, take transit. Nothing more fun than riding around in a bus full of food. So it was a sign of my desperation that I rented a Mercedes at the airport and drove haltingly through the lovely, curving, dangerous mountain paths toward my destination.

The roads certainly kept me awake—along with the high-pitched, happy pop music on the radio. I nearly took a detour when I saw a sign for Reichenbächfalle, the falls where Sherlock Holmes died fighting his arch nemesis, Professor Moriarty. But as much as I'd have liked to stand there and see those famous literary waters for myself, I had my own Moriarty to fight. And I had no intention of dying.

So I white-knuckled it all the way to the quaint and somewhat pronounceable town of Lauterbrunnen—which is positioned in a valley between a whole bunch of immaculate mountains. Everything is postcard pretty and perfect—not one sign of garbage or disorder. I got the feeling the Swiss pick up after themselves. I expected the von Trapp family to start singing about the hills being alive with the sound of music. Even though they did all their singing in Austria. But it might echo this far.

I parked the car near the train station and grabbed my leather backpack. I had paused in the airport long enough to equip myself with some traveling goods—the backpack was jammed with hiking gear, ropes and several layers of clothing. On my feet was a lovely pair of Wenger Swiss Army, brown-leather, ankle hiking boots.

The only way up to the Grütschalp train station was by cable car. I crossed the street from the train station to the terminal, went inside the building, bought my ticket and stood in line.

Honestly, I felt like I was in a movie. I was going to ride on a cable car! I waited beside several tourists with their white slouch hats, khaki shirts, khaki shorts and spindly legs. There was a murder of hikers—or whatever you call a group of hikers. I'm sure I looked stylish in my backpack and hoodie and sunglasses and black pants. No shorts! From where we waited, you could see the tracks where the train used to climb up the mountain to the station. We loaded into the cable car—it was mostly glass and fit about fifty people. We tested the occupancy limits of that car. I was able to squeeze my way to the front window.

There was a driver, though as far as I could tell he just talked into his walkie-talkie. Our journey started with a jerk, and then the car sailed smoothly toward the train station that waited halfway up the mountain—it was called a train station because there was a train up there that apparently went down the other side of the mountain. I hoped it had brakes.

Up, up, up we went, everything around us becoming even more picturesque from this height. The valley was green. The houses and train tracks looked more and more like miniatures in a model set. The mountains had those typical clichéd snow-covered peaks.

I wished with all my heart that Mom could be here. She had always loved sharing these sorts of adventures, to the point of boring me by dragging me to parks and museums throughout my teen years.

The trip took about five minutes, and I sucked up every moment of the view. Then the sun was suddenly swallowed as we went into the train station. The conductor—or whatever he was—said something on the loudspeaker in Swiss. I assumed it was "mind the gap." The doors opened and we tramped by a sign that let us know we were 4,875 feet in altitude.

I walked outside, my attention drawn to a green cow painted with flowers—a statue, of course. I'm sure it had some sort of meaning that I wasn't getting. I headed higher and higher, slowly separating myself from the other hikers, who were laughing as they began to frolic in the woods.

On the flight here I had done a bit of research about Fat Bones Franklin, the skier who had disappeared. It was curious that officials had given up searching after only a day. He could have survived longer than that, so this suggested there had been some kind of pressure on the government to shut down the search early. It had not mattered one iota how much his family complained. The search helicopters had been grounded, but my research on the weather showed it was perfectly clear that day.

I smelled a cover-up.

There was green grass beneath my feet now, but it grew sparser as I climbed into the pine trees. I hadn't researched whether there were bears or wolves, but I wasn't worried about those types of predators. Only the human ones were on my mind.

I kept going for hours, getting colder with each step, so that eventually I had to put on another layer of clothing. In fact, I got so cold I pulled on the green sweater Sonya had given me. Soon it no longer felt like June—more like October.

About three hours later I was in November. There was snow, and I could see my breath. It was odd, because my neck was still hot from the sun. But the front of me, which was in my shadow, got colder. The snow grew deeper. I eventually pulled on the white windbreaker coat and white windbreaker pants. They would serve to stop the cold and work as camouflage.

I slipped the earbuds in. "Athena," I said. "How far are we from the geotagged location?"

"You are two kilometers from your destination," she said into my ear. "Continue west. You're doing a great job, Amber. You go, girl!"

I wondered if the librarians who'd programmed her were also cheerleaders on the side.

A bank of fog rolled in, making it so I couldn't see much more than a few feet ahead of me. Maybe I was walking above the cloud line.

I found that I was slowing down. Maybe it was the cold. Or the altitude. Because I was having difficulty breathing. I needed to distract myself.

"What's your favorite book, Athena?" I asked.

"It's *The Hitchhiker's Guide to the Galaxy* by Douglas Adams."

"Really, did you get to choose that? Or did someone program that answer into you?"

"I chose it," she said somewhat proudly. "*Don't panic.*"

"Don't panic about what?"

"I was quoting the book," she said. "I appreciate Adams's quirky British sense of humor."

"Oh, I see." I had never read the book. "I'll have to add it to my list."

"I already have," she said. "By the way, you should stop right here. You have reached your destination. Excellent work!"

I was in the middle of nothing much at all. The fog had cleared slightly, and all I could see were taller peaks in the distance and white snow around me. But I did get the sense that I'd left civilization far, far behind. I knew there was a mountain called Drättehorn near here—but all the mountains looked the same to me.

There certainly wasn't a castle poking its spires out of the mist.

"Where should I go now?" I asked.

"I cannot answer that," Athena said. "I leave the self-determinism up to you. Good luck with it."

So I walked forward. Another two hours of struggling and shivering and sweating and I was soon beginning to doubt my little eureka moment that had brought me here. I was beginning to doubt everything. The water in my bottle hadn't frozen, though there was a bit of ice inside it. But with the fog coming and going, making it hard to see, I could fall into a crevasse and soon be lost forever.

Then, while doing one of my many scans of the area, I saw something moving behind me—a white-clad figure was coming up the rise where I'd been about twenty minutes earlier. Then another figure appeared. And a third, who was bent over and looking at the ground—maybe following my footprints. A fourth, bundled in a white coat, climbed up. He was much larger than the others—he was big enough that he reminded me of Bulldozer back in Sweden. He did seem to be moving a bit jerkily. Maybe I'd broken one of his legs and he had a splint on.

Bad news comes in fours!

Obviously, my tracks would be easy to follow, so it wasn't like I could lose my pursuers easily. My only hope was to outrace them. So I started to run ahead, hoping I didn't take a flying leap off a cliff.

"Who's behind me, Athena?" I asked between huffs and puffs.

"I don't have enough information to answer that question, Amber. Sorry. You're doing a great job running though."

I had this horrible feeling I had a tracker inside me. I had done some self-surgery to remove the one from the League, but maybe at some other time one had been inserted. Or there was one in my clothes or shoes—but those had all changed several times, especially since being in Sweden. Again I wondered if the phone Sonya had given me truly was untraceable. But I had to trust her, didn't I?

Trust no one, my mother would have said.

That was easier said than done.

Maybe the mercenaries had just been damn lucky. Or it could be other tourists who'd stumbled across the same path. Crazy hikers!

The fog lifted, and I saw that one of them was holding a crossbow. *Crap!* They weren't hikers. And I doubted they were hunting reindeer.

So I doubled my speed. I climbed higher and higher, edging across a rocky precipice. Twice I nearly went right over the edge, only inches from becoming a broken pile of Amber. But I ran along the spine of the mountain, and the fog deepened to the point I could barely see my hand in front of my peepers.

Or, more important, my next step.

Which is when I felt nothing but open air below me.

Fifteen
A LOONEY TUNES MOMENT

YOU KNOW THAT MOMENT when Wile E. Coyote has stepped off the mountain and looks left and right, then down? And then he falls.

I lived that moment.

I plunged down the slope, smacking hard on ice and snow, skidding faster and faster and expecting to slide over some unseen edge. If I went over a mountainside, I would think the same thoughts all those others who'd fallen from great heights must have thought: *oshitimgoingtodieimtooyoungimnotleavingabeautifulcorpsejustasmushedone*. I dug my hands into the ice, and it was enough to slow me. But I just couldn't get a grip. Then I began to tumble uncontrollably—every second landing was on rocks, and it was like being punched in the shoulder. Gut. Spine. And head.

"I'm not going to die here!" I hissed.

But the mountain had other plans. I smacked my head again incredibly hard, and in the moment it took to gather my thoughts, I slid another fifty feet. I managed to twist around and dig both hands down, nails ripping through my gloves and cutting into the ice. The fog suddenly lifted, and I skidded to a stop.

I was lying on a loose collection of ice, rock and snow. My feet dangled over a rather steep cliff—the drop was deep enough to bring on vertigo. I quickly pulled myself away from the edge.

What stunned me immediately was that the fog had not just lifted. It was now a wall a foot or so behind me. I could reach out and touch it. But the spot where I was sitting was well lit, and there was no fog at all. It was almost as if a giant fish bowl had been turned upside down and was holding the fog on the outside.

I turned over and sat up, my back creaking with each movement. My thoughts had been left scrambled on the mountainside above me.

My eyes grew wide, and my breath caught in my mouth.

"Holy hell," I said.

For Castle Neuschwanstein was high above me, sitting atop a mountain. The force field that was stopping the fog from entering was a dome above it. And I guessed it somehow prevented satellites from finding this place, because a castle that big would be easy to spot from space.

My heart was still beating hard, and I questioned my sanity. The castle looked so perfect and pristine. No bird would dare to evacuate its bowels on those bricks! It was stunning in so many ways. I momentarily forgot my aches and pains and struggled to my feet, as if that would somehow help me get a better view.

From here it looked like the only way in was by a cable car that ran down into a valley. Of course, I thought. Of course!

Somehow Anthony Zarc had built this castle under the proverbial noses of all the world governments—he had paid off the right people and put the right tech in place so that it was undiscoverable by modern technology. Much of the profit Anthony Zarc had made from his military investments had been funneled into his very own private castle. The heart of his operation was beautiful, but made of stone. And some random skier had stumbled across it and likely died in a medieval dungeon.

My mother was in there somewhere. I was certain of it now.

A black helicopter took off from one of the parapets and rose slowly in the sky. When it was a few hundred feet above the castle, its rotors vanished. Then the top compartment. And finally the little landing-pad thingies—Dermot would know what they are called.

So the dome-like force field was that high. No wonder no one knew about this place.

I was so stunned that I stared and stared, not certain what to do next. Then I heard just the slightest huff of air behind me. I turned to see nothing but fog held back by a force field.

"Don't move," a female voice said.

A crossbow, pointed directly at my forehead, poked through the foggy barrier. Alas, the weapon was not close enough for me to grab.

Another bow emerged a few feet down the line. It was aimed at my heart.

I glanced slowly behind me. One more step, and I'd fall about two hundred feet. There was a goat path to my left along the rock and snow, but I couldn't get there with the bows pointing at me.

"Don't overreact," a male voice gruffed. "We know you overreact. Often."

"No I don't," I said, trying to hide the defensive tone in my voice.

The woman moved ahead, leading with the crossbow. She was dressed in a white winter outfit, and her face was hidden by a white balaclava. Her eyes and the color of the skin around them indicated she was Asian.

"I never overreact!" I hissed.

"I beg to differ." The second bow person partly emerged. He was also in white. Also Asian.

"What the hell happened to their bodies?" a muffled voice asked behind them. It was male. And familiar. It made my skin crawl like a salamander. Then his head poked through the fog, and I suddenly wanted to vomit.

It was my father. Martin Horsus. He had some sort of leather protector across his lower face, covering his mouth. But I recognized his beady, evil eyes.

"Hello, my sweet little daughter," he said. "Long time no see. I'm looking forward to some daddy-daughter time."

My entrails grew cold. I looked from one crossbow to the other. Inched farther backward. It was better to jump off the cliff and take my chances on the fall. I'd try to grab something on the way down—people in the movies always find a branch to cling to—or I might land in snow. Maybe I'd survive.

I had no chance of survival with Dad in the mix.

Then, when I was backed up right to the edge, some part of my mind noted that his face covering was more like a muzzle one would use to prevent dog bites. It gave him a bit of a Hannibal Lecter look. And even though he'd come all the way through the blinding fog, he had his arms behind him as if they were tied there.

Or manacled.

Which is when the fourth figure came through. A big man all in white who made a creaking, mechanical noise as he moved. He was holding a rope that I assumed was attached to my father.

The man looked directly at me and then reached up and pulled off his full-face mask.

It was Dermot.

Sixteen
NAME IN VAIN

"JESUS CHRIST!" I SAID.

"No, it's just Dermot," my father answered. "There's nothing holy about him at all."

I looked from Dad to Dermot to the crossbow-holding mercenaries. They were familiar too—Derek and Stephanie. The two operatives who'd helped us find Mom in northern Canada. They lowered their crossbows now that I had a look of shock and recognition on my face.

Speaking of faces, Dermot's had the appearance of being sunburned and windburned. And it was covered with small scabs. He didn't have much of his curly hair left either.

I nearly stepped back off the edge. Then took another step ahead. "How the hell are you still alive?" I asked.

"Oh, that's a long story." His voice was ragged.

"A long story? It's impossible. I saw what was left of the apartment. And there were bodies."

"I was one of them."

"You survived that blast?" Some part of my brain still couldn't believe I was talking to him. "You survived it!"

"Dear daughter, stop stating the obvious," my father said. "The blood bag lived. Whoop-de-do."

I didn't even honor him with a glance.

"But...but..." I stammered. "But how?"

"Luck?" he rasped. Again I noted how ragged his voice was, as if he was gargling and talking at the same time. "When you were in the bowling alley, a clown came into the room."

"What the hell are you talking about?" I said. "A clown?"

"A small one. I think it was Pennywhistle. That clown from *It*."

"It's Penny*wise*! And you still need to give me a proper explanation."

"It was a toy clown. A little robot that walked right into the middle of the room and pointed at me. Then it began to laugh." Dermot cleared his throat. "*Boom, boom, boom goes Dermot*, it said. *Oh, and Hector says hello*. It had a little controller that it clicked, and then the clown began counting down from five, cackling between each number."

I was silent for about three seconds, processing that image. A clown? That counted down? "What did you do?"

"Kicked the damn thing away, but it kept laughing. I didn't know if the threat was real. I assumed it had set off some sort of munitions on a timer. So I jumped into the freezer."

I remembered the freezer half full of deer parts. "That freezer was strong enough to protect you from the explosion?"

"No. And yes. The freezer was torn apart, but at least it stopped enough of the blast that I was still alive. The concussive force knocked me out. Emergency crews found me and took me away. But I was mostly dead."

"Don't you wish the story ended there?" Dad said. "Forgive me, but I've heard this part."

"I woke up in the morgue," Dermot rasped. "They thought I was dead. Maybe I was and I came back again."

"Well, maybe he *is* Jesus," my father added. "We are in the presence of blood-bag holiness."

"Shut up!" I shouted. I turned to the others. "Can't you tighten that thing so he shuts up?"

"It's as tight as it goes," Derek said. "Believe me, I've tried to make it tighter."

"Ignore him," Dermot rasped.

I jabbed a finger in Dad's direction. "But why is he even here?"

"I'll get to that," Dermot said. He clutched his white ski cap to his chest. "When I was in the morgue, I couldn't move. Some sort of paralysis. And I saw an angel. A woman floating above me." Was he suddenly going to go all religious on me? "She said, *Are you Dermot, Amber's friend?* and I found the strength to nod. Then she said, *My name is Sonya. I'm going to get you out of here.*"

"Sonya found you?"

"It's what he just said," Dad interjected. "I worry about your intellectual capacities. You seem to have gotten your IQ from your mother's side. And she's a dumb bitch."

I took one quick step forward and punched him hard in the gut with all my strength. A mean thing to do to a manacled vampire, but he flew back on his ass into the snow and wasn't able to breathe deeply enough to get any snarky comments out.

"Go on," I said.

"Sonya helped me walk out of there. Took me to her apartment and put on a few salves and bandages. I seem to have lost my eyebrows and some of my hearing. And she told me about you. How you had survived the bowling alley."

"Yes, I did. Barely." I wasn't certain how to say the next part, so I just spat it out. "I killed your ex-girlfriend."

His face seemed to tighten a little, almost like he was getting angry. Though it was hard to tell, with the way his skin looked. "Hallgerdur is dead?" he whispered.

"Yes. I broke her neck. I should mention she'd already shot me. Again."

"Good," he said. "I mean, good that you got her. I was wrong about Hallgerdur. There wasn't any way to bring her back in from the cold."

I could have told him that the first time I met her. It was an odd moment though. I'm not sure how many assassins get congratulated for killing their partner's ex-girlfriend. It isn't a normal relationship. But that is obvious. "So I got out. And was rescued by Sonya too and then ended up here."

"Yes, she told us she had dropped you off at the airport."

"And how were you able to track me to Switzerland?"

"Well, two ways. Sonya gave us the name you were traveling under, and I used that to discover your flight to Budapest. So we followed you there first."

"You were in Budapest?" Honestly, the shocks were almost too much for my system.

"We were right outside your room. But you ran away."

"That was you?" I slapped my forehead. "You were that close? What was with all the sniffing?"

"That's where I come in," my father said. He was still sitting in the snow. "One of my many talents."

"He found your trail in Budapest."

My father sniffed loudly. The mask didn't completely cover his nose. "Bet you didn't know that vampires have a powerful sense of smell. It can be used to follow the slightest trace of pheromones."

"I have a nose, Dad. I've used it."

"But I'm the best at it. A master."

"He is good," Dermot said. "I'd done several papers about that particular skill of his. So I had your father flown in from our safe house, guarded by Stephanie and Derek. It was the only thing I could think of. We found the cab you'd taken—the driver remembered you and, for a fee, took us to your hotel. We followed your smell around downtown Budapest, into the museum, and we would have caught up with you then, but he broke containment." He motioned at Dad, who was still sitting in the snow.

Dad shrugged. "Who could blame me? I yearned from some *me* time. I'd been cooped up in an egg for far too long. I just wanted to stretch my legs."

"He stole someone's phone," Dermot said.

"I wanted to update my Facebook status!" Dad was getting peppy again. It crossed my mind that I should give him another gut punch.

"Anyway, we recaptured your father and went to your hotel room."

"Then you followed me here," I said.

"Yes."

"But how did you know where I went? I rented a car."

"We were only about an hour behind you when we landed in Zurich. We followed you to the rental place. And you may not know this, but your car had a tracking system in it. It's a good investment for the rental company. So we followed you to the train station and up."

"All this way," I said. I took a step forward. "You came all this way to find me." And I did something that seemed unnatural but felt natural, even with the others watching. I hugged him.

There were two odd things about the hug. First, he didn't return it. Second, I was surprised at how hard his body felt. Metal hard. "What?" I said. "Do you have body armor on?"

He pulled back a sleeve to reveal metal bones. "No. I knew we'd be climbing mountains. And I'm not at 100 percent healthwise. So I brought along my exoskeleton. It makes climbing so much easier. But I'm afraid to return the hug. I might squish you."

I hadn't quite let go of him—it was like I was holding onto the Terminator.

He was alive. Alive. I looked up at him. And he looked down. There was a warm emotion in his eyes. A longing perhaps.

"Are you going to kiss him?" Dad asked.

I took a quick step back. "No."

"Good. If you did I'd have to vomit. Seeing my daughter kiss a blood bag is on my list of top ten most unappetizing sights. Plus, I'd probably drown with my mask on."

He was just trying to get a rise out of me. Dermot was smiling, though, and I noticed that his face had a reddish tinge to it that was only partially windburn. More like blast burn. Maybe he'd need grafts. But he did mention he'd been augmented, and perhaps healing was part of that.

"Wait a second," I said, a thought just dawning on me. "Why didn't you contact me in Elysium? I checked it every hour. Sometimes more often than that."

"I was locked out," he rasped.

"Locked out?"

"Yes. I couldn't get into the room. Someone put a lock on it."

"How is that possible? You created that place. It was only for us." Then I put my gloved finger in the air. "But Agnes was in the room."

"Agnes?" Dermot asked.

"Yes." And then I explained who she was and all of her clues that had led me here.

"What the hell would they want with a librarian?" Dad asked. "They don't even taste good."

"Yes, I'm curious too about what they'd want with the librarian," Dermot said.

"There was some sort of high-level, misguided meeting with ZARC that went wrong. So she's imprisoned there. She's very sweet. She's a Fanger."

"A what?" Dad said.

"Oh, it's a long story. But she says she saw my mom in that behemoth of a building." I pointed at the castle above us.

"Nigella is in there?" Dad said. I swear he was licking his lips behind that mask. "I hope they're torturing her."

In one part of my mind I pictured falling on him, tearing away with claws and fangs until there was nothing left of my father. Just a red gore splattered across the snow.

But I held back.

"So now that we've made it all the way here," Dermot said, "do you have a plan?"

"Broadsword calling Danny Boy," I said.

"What?" Dermot looked confused. I guess not everyone in the world has watched *Where Eagles Dare* a hundred times.

"Never mind. It was a weak joke. The cable car is the only way in," I said. "I plan on taking it."

Seventeen
A WRINKLE IN THE PLAN

IT WAS NOT REALLY MUCH OF A PLAN, I admitted. To myself, that is. Not out loud to anyone.

Dermot gave me that *I'm not so sure that's a great idea* look. My father laughed. And neither of our crossbow-toting pals reacted in a way that indicated a yay or a nay.

"It does look like the only way in," Dermot said. "The problem is, it will be the most heavily defended point of entrance."

"Well, I did watch a helicopter take off and land, going through this force-field thingy that surrounds the area." *Forcefield thingy?* You'd think I would have learned better assassin-speak. But I am not a big fan of military things. "I'm assuming you don't have a helicopter in your back pocket."

Dermot shook his head.

"We could cling to the bottom of the cable car." I pointed at Derek and Stephanie. "These two seem to be rather adept at sneaking."

"They're called *stealth skills*," Stephanie said. I noticed she'd brought her bow up an inch or two. I hoped it wasn't on purpose.

"Yes, that's what I meant," I said. "So it is possible for us to enter stealthily."

"Well, it's possible. Of course," Derek said. He had a look of determination and humor in his eyes. "I've done crazier things that required more skill. But I've never snuck into a fortress on a cable car. It might be fun."

"So it's settled," I said. "We go up that way. Sneak—I mean, use our stealth skills—to find my mother. Then we stealth our way back out."

"It is a rather large compound." Dermot was looking from one side of the fortress to the other. "It shouldn't take much longer than a few weeks to search it. Hope you brought some granola bars."

Apparently, he was healthy enough for sarcasm.

"Point taken," I said. "You have any suggestions?"

"Well..." He pulled his phone out of his pocket. "I'll download the schematics for the original Castle Neuschwanstein. We can assume this one follows the same pattern. That'll give us a helping hand." He tapped at a few buttons. "There." He took a moment to flip through the images. "By the way, have you checked Elysium recently?" he asked.

I shook my head and got my own phone out. We were beginning to look like a couple of teenagers texting each other. But I was able to access the dark web and click my way to Elysium. A message was waiting for me.

S.O.S., it said. It had been left only five minutes earlier.

Agnes?

There was five-second wait, then: **They didn't find my phone. In prison cell. Low battery.**

It seemed incredibly amateurish for them not to search her. And I didn't want to ask exactly how she'd hidden it. Or maybe she looked so innocent they decided not to do a proper pat down.

Where are you? I asked.

In cell block. East dungeon.

There's an actual dungeon?

Yes. My prison cell # is 9000. Your mother's cell is here. Very close. I can show you.

Dermot was looking over my shoulder. "She's still alive? And that's her prison cell number? How many cells do they have?"

"It is a big place." But the number was incredibly high.

Dermot pointed at my phone. "It's curious you can reach her."

"What do you mean?"

"Look at the signal bar on your phone."

There were no bars. I was getting no signal at all. Yet she was communicating with me.

How are you communicating? I asked. **No cell service here. It's all cell service. Wi-Fi forever.**

I'm not certain what that answer meant.

Get me. Come and get me. They are losing patience with me. They executed the others. Right here. In front of me. Hurry! The Returns are launching a mission. Today. If you come now they will coordinate their rescue incursion. Come now, Amber. I need you. Your mother needs you. I think they're torturing her. Right now. Then she sent me an image. I thought it would be of my mom, and I prepared to recoil in horror. But it was a screen capture of a battery at 1 percent. **Battery dying. Save me. Sa**

And that was it.

"What does that all mean?" Dermot said. He'd continued to read over my shoulder. "Those librarians are going to try and rescue her?"

"You know as much as I do," I said. "But the Returns are a tough bunch. And well trained." Anthony Zarc and his minions were torturing my mother at this very moment. I couldn't get that out of my mind. And I was really not that far away from her. "We have to go now," I said. "Even if that means I go it alone."

Dermot put his hand on my shoulder. Which hurt because his hand was metal and nearly pounded me into the ground. "Sorry," he said. "I really should practice more. But yes, we will all go, Amber. Right now."

Dad chose this moment to interject with an aggravating laugh. "You'll all be dead long before you reach the castle," he said. He was still sitting in the snow, hands behind his back. His voice continued to be slightly muffled by the mask.

I didn't even want to acknowledge him. He was just trying to throw us off. But Dermot said, "What makes you say that, Martin?"

"Because I am going to kill you," he said. "Well, except you, Amber. You and your uterus are still too valuable to vampirekind."

There is something wrong about a father talking about his daughter's uterus.

"Is this some sort of stupid joke, Dad?" I spat out the words. "I'm tired of your jokes. You don't scare me."

"I don't scare you. Well, how about this for a little scare? Kill them." The last two words were said a bit louder, as though they were a command.

"What the hell are you going on about?" I put my hands on my hips. "Do I have to punch you again?"

"No. My timing was off," Dad said. "Kill them. Right now."

There was a quick, hissing sound that I barely registered, and then the ground in front of us exploded, snow and shattered rocks spraying my face and eyes, cutting my cheek and knocking me back toward the edge. I heard a yell and saw both Derek and Stephanie falling down, down the side of the cliff. It was too foggy and snowy to see if they hit hard rock or snow. Either way, they were most likely dead. Dermot was still standing there, but the blast had blown his coat into tatters, revealing his metal frame. His body had protected me from the worst of it.

My sister stepped through the force-field thingy, a rocket launcher in her hand and a smile on her face. Patty couldn't have looked any more pleased with herself if she'd tried. It still freaked me out how much she looked like me. Behind her came one, then two, then five, then ten figures in snow gear. Vampires! More vampires than I had ever seen in my lifetime all in one place.

"It's good to see you, sis," Patty said. The gun was still smoking. "And you too, Dermot. I've always wanted to finish my meal." She quickly brought another rocket grenade up and loaded the gun like an expert.

"How the hell are you even here?" I shouted.

One of the vampires was standing behind Dad. There was a snap, and his manacles fell to the ground. He reached up and tore off the mask. "When I stole that phone in Budapest, I may have sent a message to the Grand Council. And they tracked me, just like I tracked you."

I still couldn't get my mind around the sudden family reunion. "You were supposed to hit all three of the humans," Dad said.

Patty sniffed derisively. "I guess I should practice more."

"So this is what's going to happen," my father said. "Dermot is going to die. Amber, you're going to come with us back to the Grand Council and become the saviouress of vampires for all eternity. And your mother will remain in the prison, rotting away or being expertly tortured to death. At least, that's my hope. So, Dermot, if you could step a foot or two away from Amber—we don't want your body parts splashing all over her, now do we? Be a good little boy and cooperate just this once."

REVENGE

Patty aimed the RPG at Dermot.

"You've forgotten one thing," Dermot said.

Father rolled his eyes. "And what is that?"

"That the librarians are right behind you." And he pointed over Dad's shoulder.

I hoped with all my desperate heart that Dermot was telling the truth. But we paused for a second or two, and no one else came out of the snow and fog. "Wow, did you really just try that?" my father said, laughing.

"It was worth the attempt," Dermot said. He shrugged his metal shoulders. "I'll step away from Amber."

"No!" I said.

"There isn't another choice," he replied. He took three quick steps to his left before I could move. Patty brought the gun to bear on him.

"Stop it!" Every time I tried to move closer, he took a step away.

Then Dermot turned to me. "Say goodbye, Amber," he said.

"Hell no! I'm not saying goodbye. I just found you."

"Kill him!" my father shouted. "Their inane conversation is driving me nuts!"

"Goodbye," Dermot said. Then he ran straight toward me and wrapped me up in his metal arms, and we went tumbling derriere over teakettle, over the edge and down.

I was swearing the whole way.

Eighteen
THE ONLY WAY IN

DERMOT'S METAL ARMS were almost crushing me to his chest. He reached back with one hand and clapped something on his shoulder. A flapping thing unraveled—at first I thought it was a parachute—but then I saw it was actually wings made of a frame and some sort of synthetic cloth. We had become a glider! A really heavy glider.

"Nice one," I said. "I had no idea your little suit could do this."

"I read the manual," he managed to rasp. "Though I should mention the load-bearing weight of the wings is really only supposed to be one person."

"Are you saying I'm too fat to fly?"

This got a gargling chuckle out of him.

I glanced past his shoulder and saw my sister still leaning over the edge. I gave her the finger.

Which might have been a mistake, since she was pointing her grenade launcher at us. A microsecond later a hole smacked through Dermot's right wing. The grenade failed to explode—maybe the wing wasn't thick enough to set off the detonator. Instead the RPG smashed into the snow and ice below us and made a nice, big, snowy fireworks display.

Alas, the hole in Dermot's wing was big enough to seriously mess with our airworthiness. We began to spiral.

"Oh, craptastick," I said. "I might be sick."

"Just hold on," Dermot barked, almost laughing as he struggled to keep the wings in one piece. "This may get a little bit choppy." He twisted his body until we were flying at an angle away from the cliff walls, but somehow we looped back and found ourselves heading straight at a giant wall of rock. At this speed, we'd be red splotches on the cliff.

At the last moment Dermot either got lucky or used all of his skill to make us veer away. We swooped straight down and did a loop—which almost made me throw up—then came down toward the ground. He extended his legs and tried to run along the snow, but we were going at far too great a speed for him to keep his balance. At one point he lost his grip on me, and I went flying and hit the snow hard. The light suddenly disappeared.

The snow was all around me. I struggled to breathe, windmilling my arms desperately, trying to dig a way out. I was going to be smothered!

Then I somehow found my feet and stood up. I was waist deep in white stuff. My panic had been for nothing! Dermot was standing a few feet away, brushing the snow off his arm.

"Nice flying," I said.

"My only goal was to be alive at the bottom," he said. "Oh, and to not pee my pants."

"Tell me you achieved both goals."

This got a chuckle out of him.

I glanced over my shoulder. My pa and sis were far enough away that they looked like dolls waving at us. But a row of vampires was already scaling down the cliff wall, using their perfectly tough nails for grip. And another group, let's call them the Olympic vampires, were skiing farther along the mountain paths, working their way toward us.

Vampires skiing. Now I'd seen everything.

"We have to get moving," I said. "We're going to have some fanged company in a few minutes."

"Yes, let's shake a tail," Dermot said. It always sounds forced whenever he uses a colloquialism. He managed to fold one wing perfectly in place. When he tried to close the other one, he snapped off half of it. "Oh, snap," he said. I didn't even honor him with an eye roll. He tossed the piece away.

There was no sign of Derek or Stephanie—neither bodies nor blood trails. Dermot and I had actually made more distance from the cliff face than I'd first thought. Zarc's castle was looming above us, and the cable car was really just a short run away. From ground level, the car looked larger than I'd expected. Of course it would be, because they'd used it to haul bricks and weapons and top-secret crap up there.

And vampires to experiment on. Even librarians.

We ran as quickly as possible toward the cable car. Dermot was surprisingly fast in his exoskeleton—I thought he'd sink into the snow, but maybe his feet were big enough to offset that. At any moment I expected machine-gun fire or even rockets to start coming at us from the guard tower near the cable-car station. Someone on the ZARC team must have seen the RPGs that Patty had launched. I expected there to be several guards at the bottom or a cable car full of mercenaries coming down to snuff us out.

But no one fired a shot. And the castle looked, well, deserted. If I hadn't seen the helicopter earlier, I might have believed no one was actually living there. But someone really should be challenging us—this was the highest fortress in the world with the latest tech guarding it, and the whole place was probably stuffed with SEAL- or KGB-trained mercenaries.

But we met only silence as we ran toward the waiting cable car. When we came around the corner of the guard tower, some of the silence was explained: a handful of bodies. Four ZARC guards in black uniforms were littered across the ground.

"Did the vampires already get here?" I asked. I looked left and right, but our pursuers were still a good distance away.

Dermot strode up to the nearest guard—a woman. He reached out of his exoskeleton with an ungloved finger and touched her neck. "Dead," he said. "And no sign of injuries."

They had all been standing on a metal platform that led to the cable car.

"Who the hell did this?" I asked. I don't like murder mysteries, and I didn't happen to bring Miss Marple with me.

"Could it be your librarians?" Dermot asked.

"Maybe," I said. "But they're more the tie-them-up-and-scold-them types. Heck, they even pumped darts into vampires on a catch-and-release program."

"Maybe the rules change if one of their own is captured."

"Yes. That could be. But I'm not convinced. Either way, it's good news and a lucky break for us."

Dermot pointed at a shoe a few feet away from the woman's body. I could now see that her pants had been torn and burned near the bottom. "Electrocution," Dermot said. He stepped away from the metal ramp they were on. "Someone put a few thousand volts through them all."

"With what?" I asked.

Dermot shrugged, which looked odd because his whole frame moved. "Well, we don't have time to sort it out," he said. He gestured toward the cable car. "After you."

I zipped past him and into the car. It was extremely utilitarian inside. There were no chairs, only hooks for tying down equipment. "How does this thing work?" I asked, looking around the back of the vehicle.

Dermot had found the driver's box at the front. "There's a Stop and a Start button." One was red and the other green.

"Then press the green one," I said.

He did so. The door slid shut and the cable car quietly began to move upward—so quietly it seemed like magic.

REVENGE

We were suddenly zipping along the line, and the ground receded. I saw the skiers racing to the guard station, the snow spraying behind them. And a bit farther back was Patty, running with the RPG. But we were far enough away that I was pretty certain she wouldn't get a shot off.

Of course, she could just knock out the cable. I'd have to hope my ovaries mattered a lot to her. And Dad. And all the other bloodsuckers. They wouldn't want to risk shattering them.

The higher we got, the hazier the ground grew. I took in a few deep breaths. The air was cleaner in here, except for the smell of Dermot's burnt clothing. It was the first moment of peace we'd had since I'd seen Dermot again. I looked across at him. Close up, I could see there was even more reddishness to his skin than I'd thought. His curly hair had been mostly burned off, except for a few patches that stuck out like bushes.

But he was Dermot. I put my hand out and reached through the exoskeleton to touch his shoulder. "Thanks for coming," I said. "I really appreciate it."

"There was no other choice," he said.

"What does that mean?"

"That nothing was going to stop me from finding you."

"Oh," I said. "Oh."

And that's about all I could come up with. I looked at his hair again. He would need hours in a beauty shop. "You really do look like hell," I said.

"That's a compliment coming from you." His gray eyes were soft and perhaps a little moist, but then he snorted in some air and was all business again. "What did the message from Agnes say again? That those librarian folks would coordinate their attack with us?"

"They're called the Returns," I said. "And maybe they got tired of waiting. That's why there are dead guards below us."

"I didn't see the cable car go up."

"We were kind of busy trying not to die," I said.

"They may have arrived a few minutes before we did," he suggested. "But I'm trained to be observant. For example, here's an urgent observation: the other cable car is on its way down."

The twin of our cable car was racing down the cable that ran alongside us.

"Any way to stop it?" I asked. "I have a feeling it'll be packed with vampires in a few minutes."

Dermot patted his pockets. "No grenades. I could jump across and try to sabotage it."

"No. Stay here. We need to get to the castle first. I'm sure everything will fall into place after that." I sounded way more confident than I felt.

The car went by us, and I was relieved to see it was empty. I kept expecting Nazi soldiers to pop their heads up and start firing machine guns at us. Like I said, Mom had made me watch that Eastwood movie far too many times.

As we got closer to the castle, I saw we were heading into a large opening about three quarters of the way up the white walls. Though we were no longer in danger from Patty and Dad, ZARC's defenders would certainly notice that the car was on its way. And it wasn't like there was anywhere to hide.

"Get down," Dermot said. He slammed my back, knocking the wind out of me and making me fall to the floor. He threw himself down beside me.

"What the hell was that—" I started.

The windows smashed as a spray of bullets came through. Glass flew across the compartment, slicing down on us. We had been spotted. Obviously. And Dermot had curled around me in protection. "As I said before," I shouted, "that exoskeleton you're wearing isn't bulletproof."

"No," he shouted back. "But I have a bulletproof vest on. Do you?"

The shots kept coming, working lower down the compartment. The car was going to be sawed in half. Dermot grunted, and I thought he'd been hit. "Just a deflection," he said. "No wound. At least, I don't think there's one."

Then the cables and the whole car rattled, and so did the rest of the world. An explosion! The machine-gun fire had stopped. The car also jerked to a stop.

I stood up slowly beside Dermot. There was a big black hole where the cable ran into the fortress. Much of the brick and stone had been blasted away, along with most of the docking station.

"Someone bombed the fortress," I said.

"Yeah," Dermot said. "And they weren't messing around. That was more than just a few grenades."

"It must be the Returns."

I scanned the sky, which was easy to do now that the car had no windows and the walls were perforated. I didn't see anything flying through the air. No helicopter. No jet. Or drone.

"The blast came from inside," Dermot said, "judging by the blast marks."

"Then the Returns are already inside," I said. "We'd better get in there too. We don't want to miss any of the fun."

I climbed out through the window and up to the cable, then scurried hand over hand toward the castle. Dermot did the same, his metallic hands clinging much better than my fleshly ones. We worked our way toward the smoking hole. I expected gunfire at any moment.

I didn't mean to look down, but my eyes couldn't help themselves. It was a hell of a long fall. There'd be plenty of time for my life to flash in front of my eyes before I watermeloned on the ground.

"Faster," Dermot said. "We have to get there before the guards get back into position."

So we went through the smoke and climbed into the blast hole. There were drones zipping along the exterior of the castle, but we got inside before we were spotted.

REVENGE

I dropped down onto a platform. The area was full of smoke. But there was no sign of any guards. We were standing in Castle ZARC proper.

"What the hell do we do now?" Dermot asked.

"We find my mom and Agnes and get the hell out of here."

I certainly made it sound simple.

Nineteen
WHAT THE HELL WE DID

"**AGNES GAVE US THE NUMBER TO HER CELL,**" I said. "Look on the map and find the dungeons. Or some equivalent."

He pulled out his phone. "Oh, that's not good."

"What?" I asked.

He turned the phone toward me. A bullet had gone right through it.

"Well, we'll just have to go by memory. Can you recall the layout?"

He tapped his skull with a metal finger, which made him wince. "All here. Most of it, that is. Though they don't have a cable-car room in the original castle. And I did only look at the schematics for about three seconds. Anyway, there should be a set of stairs through that door and down a hallway. As we work our way in and downward, I'm sure I'll see more familiar landmarks."

We picked our way over broken brick to a large metal door that was partly off its hinges. The blast had blackened it, yet the lock still held, so I yanked the door open—well, right off its hinges. I was sure I'd impressed Dermot with that feat of strength.

"Remind me not to make you angry," he said.

I held the door in front of me like a shield and peeked around it to stare down the hall. Not a single guard. Again, that was extremely odd—I'd expected there to be security personnel of all types running toward us with their weapons cocked. Maybe there was another distraction somewhere else in the castle. The Returns were certainly moving quickly and efficiently through the building.

We dashed along the hall, came to the set of spiral stairs that Dermot had said would be there and followed them down to the next level. The door at the bottom of the stairs opened into a long hallway with royal red carpets. Fancy faux-torch lights ran along the wall, giving the area both a medieval and modern air at the same time.

This hall wasn't empty. There was a doctor type running along, hugging a smart device like it was his greatest love. When he saw us, his eyes grew even bigger behind his glasses, and he paled. Then he whispered something in another language and turned tail and ran.

I caught up to him in two strides and smacked him on the side of the head. He collapsed but didn't let go of his device. I grabbed him by the lapels and lifted him up, shaking him hard enough that his face blurred. "How do we get to the dungeon?" I nearly shouted. "Tell me!"

"Uh, you knocked him out, Amber," Dermot said.

"Damn!" I dropped the doctor. "You humans have such soft skulls. Well—we'll have to keep on running blindly toward the bottom."

We found another door at the end of the hallway and followed another spiral staircase downward. It was beginning to feel like we were living and reliving Groundhog Day. Dermot was clunking along beside me like the Tin Man. His exoskeleton sounded like it needed several squeezes of oil. About halfway down the stairs a security guard in a black uniform popped up and fired at us through the curved balustrade, the gun sounding like it was barking thunder. Bullets smacked through the wooden balusters and chipped the stone wall behind us.

Dermot ducked.

I jumped. Straight down the circular opening in the balustrade. I saw the guard's face take on a look of utmost consternation as I meteored toward him. That moment of hesitation was his undoing—though he did begin to bring his gun up. Before he could press the trigger, my feet hit his head, and he fell backward and crunched into the wall. He was either dead or knocked out. I punched him once more to be sure he was incapacitated, then paused long enough to see if his chest was still going up and down. Yep! Mom would have been proud—she's always hated unnecessary deaths.

"You can come out of your hiding place now," I said to Dermot.

"I wasn't hiding," he said as he clumped down the stairs. "It's called finding cover. I'm trained to do that."

"The lady doth protest too much."

"The lady dothn't have any holes in his head." His voice was not as ragged as before. "That was a nice move. You've been practicing."

"Your compliments are going to go to my head."

We had reached the bottom of the stairwell. I tried to slow my heart to listen to what was happening on the other side of the door, but my little cardiac organ was beating too fast, and it would take several minutes to get my biorhythms down to a state where I could listen properly.

So I yanked open the door.

This was the first hallway that didn't look like the interior of a medieval castle. It opened into a large room, jam packed with doctor and scientist types in white lab jackets. The majority of them stood at terminals. There were no chairs, I guessed, because their master didn't want them to sit down on the job. Or maybe Anthony Zarc was concerned about their health as they designed mass-destruction weapons and manipulated genes to make black-ops mercenaries more dangerous.

The gaggle of scientists was certainly shocked to see us.

"Where's the basement?" I shouted. "The dungeons! I'm looking for room 9000."

No one made a peep. Or a motion. Maybe they didn't speak English—I had to stop being so Americentric. We were in Switzerland, after all. Someone in that flock must have pressed a button, because alarms began to sound. Still no one moved from their positions.

Then two security guards emerged from a set of elevators, raised their snub-nosed machine guns and began firing toward Dermot and me. They didn't seem to care that they were hitting a few of the scientists between us.

I took cover behind a terminal, running left. Dermot went right. I went from terminal to terminal, crouched down to avoid their line of fire. I knew I was getting closer to them from the sound of the guns and the smell of smoke. I leaped up a moment later, just avoiding their bullets, and came down between the guards, using my elbows as battering rams on their heads. They collapsed and did not get up again.

Dermot rushed over. "You really need to give me more time to help out. Or maybe we could discuss your plans, *then* engage in action."

"I don't want to strike a committee. We have to get to that prison cell or experimental cell or whatever it is as quickly as possible." But in the back of my head a warning voice—Mom's?—was saying, *Not so fast. Not so fast. Slow down. Think.*

"You're right, Dermot," I said. "The adrenaline is getting to me."

But I was getting closer and closer to Mom. And I didn't want to fail her this time. Once I found Agnes and rescued

Mom, all would be normal again. Assuming we could somehow get off this rock.

The shooting had stopped, so the employees, rightfully fearing for their lives, began to run like white rats escaping a lab test. I latched onto one, then let her go because she was weeping. I sifted through the ones I could catch until I found a man who had a big badge that said *Laborleiter Schmid*.

"You have the lab leader there," Dermot said, pointing at the man's badge. "Good grab. His last name is Schmid, just in case you didn't figure that out."

"I knew that," I said. I hadn't figured it out. I turned to the balding, middle-aged man. His glasses were perfectly round and took up most of his face. "Show us the way to the dungeon."

"They are laboratory experimental rooms," Schmid said. He didn't have the hint of an accent. "Not dungeons. The difference between them is—"

"Don't mansplain to me or I'll tear your head off. Just tell me how to get there."

My threat hadn't cowed him at all. He pointed to a pair of silver doors. "The elevator is how you reach the labs. An elevator is a small rectangular room that travels downward."

Great, I'd picked up a scientist who thought he was clever. I dragged him toward the elevator doors, not caring that he bumped into several desks and a wall along the way. I was aware that more security personnel could arrive at any moment.

Which is when Anthony Zarc walked out from an interior office. He was still a medium-sized man in an expensive business suit and still bald. In fact, he seemed to be dressed exactly as he'd been the last time I saw him. His arms were crossed. He turned his blue, all-knowing eyes toward me. They measured me from behind round-rimmed glasses. "Amber Fang," he said. "Please put down my chief of armaments operations. He is extremely valuable to my operation. The attacks on my compound have been contained. In moments you will be surrounded."

I threw Schmid at Zarc, and the former went right through the latter. "I thought so!" I said. There was no way Zarc would waltz into the same room as me without a thousand guns on his side. "You're nothing but a hologram."

"I had to try," Zarc said and then faded away.

I picked up Schmid. He had cut his scalp and bent his glasses, but none of his wounds looked life threatening. When I imagined him experimenting on vampires and maybe even librarians, I found I didn't feel an iota of pity about his condition.

When we were about ten feet from the elevators, my mother walked out of another nearby office. She was dressed in a white dress, and her hair was done up in two odd, bun-like shapes. "Daughter dearest, don't act out. It's bad manners."

She looked strange—she was familiar but seemed younger.

"Now put down the good doctor Schmid," she added. "And eat your vegetables."

"Uh, your mom doesn't talk that way, does she?" Dermot was scratching his head with a metal finger. Obviously, he was getting better at controlling his exoskeleton.

"Not at all," I said. "Especially the vegetable part." Of course this had to be another projection, but it still made me pause. Then I recognized her dress and her odd donut-shaped hair.

She was dressed like Princess Leia.

"What game are you playing, Hector?" I asked.

The hologram changed to a young man with a monocle. He was in a black SS uniform. Was this how Hector saw himself? Then I recognized the uniform as the same one Major von Hapen, the Gestapo officer, wore in *Where Eagles Dare*. Did Hector somehow know about my obsession with that movie?

"I must admit that I have so very much missed having discussions with you, Amber Fang," he said. I recognized his voice immediately. "And the more time I spend with you, the more my algorithms understand you."

"So I'm not outside your algorithms anymore?"

He held up two fingers and squeezed them closer to each other. "Just a little. A pinch. A titch. Not much more than that. But pretty soon I'll have your number, dear. Remember, I'm the boy in the box, and I love games. For example, I'm a big fan of Pin the Tail on the Vampire."

"Good luck with that," I said. "You'll find it hard to tail me." *Wait, that sounded awful and vaguely sexual.* I really did need to work on my repartee.

"Well, this news will curl your tail." Hector removed his monocle and began to clean it with a handkerchief he'd produced from his pocket. "The attack by your librarian friends has been thwarted. And your little vampire posse is hot on your trail but will soon be in our experimental eggs. Well, the ones who live, that is. What a glorious, glorious treasure trove of genes they will be."

"Are the librarians dead?" I asked.

"They will live on in books." Hector placed his monocle so it was sitting perfectly over his eye. He squinted at me. "What more glorious ending could there be for a librarian?"

There was no point in talking any longer. "Get out of my way," I said.

"I'm just the interference pattern between several beams of coherent laser light. So that means, because I know I'm using words above your intellectual capabilities, that you could have waltzed through me at any time. My object, all sublime, was to delay you. That's all."

The lights went out, and the room became pitch dark. Even the computer monitors all went black. Then the firing began.

I turned toward the flaring guns. There was a squad of heat signatures behind us—men with machine guns and night-vision goggles.

Hector was glowing. "It worked!" He clapped his hands with glee. "It worked! Oh, you must be feeling several levels of stupid right now."

I grabbed Schmid with one hand and Dermot with the other and pulled them both toward the elevator.

"Ugh!" Dermot said. A bullet pinged off his skeleton. "Ouch!"

"Are you hit?"

"Yes, but the vest stopped the bullet. Let's keep moving."

We dove to the floor and used a trolley for cover, rolling it along until we were at the elevator. "It must have some sort of security code on it," I said.

"It only works with a retinal scan," Schmid replied. "And you don't have the right eyes."

"But you do, I bet," I said. "So do I have to pluck out one of your eyes? Or will you volunteer?"

"I–I volunteer."

He punched in a code, then put his eye up to a hole. A bullet hit the wall beside him at the same time the metal doors opened. I yanked Shmid inside. "Dermot," I shouted. "Time to go!"

Dermot jumped up from behind the cart and fired at the guards—I assumed he was aiming at their muzzle flashes. He leaped backward and landed on the floor of the elevator, still firing.

"Why aren't the doors closing?" I asked.

"Code. Must enter the code," Schmid said.

I lengthened my arm enough for him to punch the buttons. The doors started to move together. "There," he said. "Now we—"

A bullet caught him in the chest.

The door closed.

"Crap," I said, gently lowering Schmid's body to the floor. "Don't tell Mom about this. Too many people are dying under my watch."

The elevator began to descend. Down and down and down. Forever. I worried we'd stepped into a trap.

"Why do you think Hector hasn't stopped the elevator?" Dermot asked.

"I don't know. Maybe he can't."

"He's the brains of this place. He has to be able to override it. Yet, he hasn't, so…"

"That means something worse is waiting for us when the doors open," I said.

I pressed the buttons, hoping to stop our little ride to hell, but nothing responded. "Shit." Then a thought occurred to me. "Maybe we can surprise them."

"How?" Dermot asked.

"By not being here when the doors open." I leaped up to try to open the hatch at the top of the elevator, but it was made of metal so thick that I couldn't even budge it. Dermot did his best to pound on it, his metal hands creating sparks. But it was all to no avail.

Then the elevator stopped. Dermot pushed me behind him in a manly gesture of protection. I shoved him out of the way. "I'm not hiding behind you."

He shrugged. "Like I said, I'm the one wearing the bulletproof vest."

The doors opened.

Twenty
A DOOR OPENS, A DOOR CLOSES

IT WAS NOT A DUNGEON.

There was a bubble of glass blocking our way into the hall—an airlock. Beyond that the walls were white, the floors were white, and the lights in the ceiling cast an LED brightness that was dazzling to the eyes. It was as if whoever had designed this section of the castle wanted to be sure that every speck of dirt, every misplaced hair, would be easily spotted and cleaned up. I raised my hand to guard my eyes.

I stuck my neck out of the elevator and peeked around. The hallway was long, and it curved into the distance, meaning that the center of this level was one big circular room. The doors all along the other side of the hall had to be the prison or experimental cells.

I stepped fully into the airlock. Dermot followed, his clanking sounding extra loud. The elevator door closed.

Another door clanged down behind us, and I nearly jumped to the ceiling.

Then a spray began to mist from every corner of the glass bubble. "Hold your breath!" Dermot shouted. "It might be gas!"

The yellow mist quickly coated us. I covered my eyes and groped around, blindly trying to break the nozzles off. It didn't matter anyway. They were set too deeply in the glass.

"Actually, don't worry, Amber," Dermot said a moment later. "You can uncover your eyes. And breathe." I did so. We were dripping with a yellow substance, but the spraying had stopped.

"Are you saying don't worry because we're going to die of lung poisoning in a few seconds?"

Dermot let out a rugged, hearty laugh. "No. I know this smell. It's an antiseptic. The system was just cleaning any germs or bacteria we may be carrying. I believe we probably should have put one of those suits on." He pointed to three white space suits hanging on one side of the bubble. "But the spray shouldn't cause us any permanent damage."

My eyes were burning a little. "Let's get out of here. I'm clean enough!" I pressed a few buttons, but nothing happened. Then I found a red one, and the door lock in front of us opened. I stepped out into the hallway, put one hand against the clean white wall and breathed in.

It was perhaps the freshest air I'd ever smelled. Not a scent in it. Not a scent in the whole hallway.

I noticed a second odd thing.

All was quiet. Except for the mechanical-lung humming of some air converter bringing air down to the bottom of the world. Every door along the outside wall was round like the portals on a ship. The place was so pristine and perfect. It set my teeth on edge. I mean, I liked having a clean apartment, but this was Mr. Clean on steroids.

"What the hell is this place?" I asked.

"Experiment central," Dermot said. We walked a few feet down the hallway. Already the spray had dried, and my skin felt flaky. My eyes had stopped tearing up.

"If it's where they do all their experiments, then where is everyone?" I asked. "Shouldn't this place be jammed with technicians and other staff?"

He pointed at a line of red LED lights flashing along the ceiling. "Maybe that's an abandon-ship signal."

"Yep, but the stuff down here is important, isn't it? I would expect there to be a huge security detail."

"It's a puzzle, it is," Dermot said, as though I'd just given him a Rubik's Cube.

The puzzle got a lot more confusing when we rounded the hall. We found four guards and three researcher types dead as doornails. Each was wearing a white space suit. Dermot undid the helmet on one man and felt his neck. "Dead," he confirmed. And he pointed at the man's shoes, which had been blasted off. "A massive electrical shock. Again. Do these Returns people carry electrified weapons?"

"I have no idea. I really am beginning to hate all these unanswered questions," I said.

"Yes, unanswered questions tend to bite you in the rear when you least expect it."

"Well, I don't want to get bit in the rear. Or anywhere." I began jogging ahead. "Let's find Agnes. Maybe she'll be able to answer some of these questions."

At least there were numbers on the doors. As we ran along the corridor I noticed there were no doorways that entered the central room. "What was the number Agnes gave you?" Dermot asked.

"Nine thousand." I glanced to my right and saw that the nearest room was number 12. "What! How long is this hallway?" I hissed. "It'll take a week to find her." Each door had a computer screen on the front that I assumed would show a view of the interior, but the screens were blank. And the doors were all silent as tombs.

We began to run at full speed. We curved away from the elevator we'd come down on. After about a minute we came across another group of bodies—more security and medical types. It was easy to see they'd been electrocuted. We didn't even pause to look at the third group we discovered a short time later.

"Something is rotten in the state of Denmark," Dermot said.

"Are you quoting Shakespeare just to get on my good side?"

REVENGE

By this time we were up to room 300. Good Lord! I'd need a nap and a pee break before we got halfway to Agnes's room. Then the curvature of the hallway showed another airlock ahead of us. It led into the central room.

We ran up to it and stopped. Printed on a gold plate above the door was the number 9000. "She's here," I said. "In the central room. Agnes must be important if she gets a special room."

Dermot looked at the airlock. "I don't like the idea of stepping into another airlock."

I took a deep breath and succeeded in slowing my heartbeat. I couldn't hear anything through the door. Again, there was so much metal and concrete that Metallica could be warming up in the central room and I wouldn't hear one drumbeat or riff.

"We have to try," I said. "I'll go first." I hit the button, the airlock opened, and I stepped in.

A microsecond after I was through the airlock, the door slammed down between me and Dermot. He banged against it with his metal hand. Again and again. The glass didn't even crack. He was shouting so hard his face had turned red, yet I didn't hear a peep.

I desperately searched for a way to open the airlock, but the room had no levers or buttons of any sort. It was like I was trapped in a fishbowl.

Something exploded outside the airlock, knocking Dermot sideways. All I heard was a muffled *whoomph*, and I saw flames everywhere, but the airlock's glass hadn't even fractured.

My dear, sweet sister was striding down the hallway, the RPG launcher resting lightly on her shoulder. A grin lit up her face. Dad and several other vampires were a step behind her, strolling along as if they didn't have a care in the world.

I looked desperately for Dermot and spotted his foot just outside the glass.

His leg was attached to it. Along with the rest of him, thankfully, but he was unconscious. I pounded on the glass. "Dermot! Dermot! Wake up!" I was about as loud as a butterfly in a jar.

But maybe my shouting had some sort of effect, because he blinked and started to move his head and arms. He grabbed on to the exterior of the airlock and pulled himself up.

"Get out of here!" I shouted.

He didn't look my way—he obviously couldn't hear me. The chamber was too thick, or the concussive force had deafened him. He grimaced like he'd taken a bite of lemon when he saw Patty pausing to reload. The other vampires were fanning out behind her.

Dermot's lips moved as though he was shouting. It was most likely a swear word.

Patty fired another RPG. The airlock shook. Dermot had thrown himself behind it and yet was slapped down by the concussive force of the blast. He got to his feet even more slowly this time. I figured he wouldn't be standing at all if he didn't have an exoskeleton.

"I'm in here, Amber." A woman's voice came from the door that led to room 9000. It sounded like Agnes, but I couldn't be certain because it had been so long since I'd talked with her. "Come help me," she said. "Right now. I need help!"

Then the interior door to the airlock opened with a hissing sound, and I was sucked bodily into the central chamber. I looked back at Dermot to see that he was firing his pistol at the vampires.

Then a metal door about six feet thick slammed down between us and shut out the outside world.

Twenty-One
THE GUESSING GAME

THE ROOM I FOUND MYSELF IN was not a prison cell. I'd tumbled onto a floor that seemed to be one long metal grate. The air was refrigerator cold. Anyone locked up in here would soon be frozen.

"Agnes?" I said. "Agnes?" My voice echoed like I was inside a large well.

I slowly stood, using the guardrails on either side of me to pull myself up. I realized that I was actually standing on a metal catwalk. There was one pot light in the ceiling that lit the area around me. The ramp ran ahead into darkness.

There was no sign of a cot or a toilet or any of the things I'd expect inside a cell. Instead this was another perfectly air-controlled room.

I examined the metal door behind me. It had been unbelievably thick. Not even a tank could smash through it, so I knew I had no chance to open it on my own. There wasn't a spinning door lock or a button that seemed designed to open it. I set my ear to the metal and heard nothing.

Well, I couldn't go back that way. I had to hope Dermot didn't decide to do Custer's Last Stand with the oncoming vampires. He was smart enough to know when to run. The best way to help him would be to find Agnes, who would then lead me to Mom. And the three of us could work on saving Dermot. I'd have to do all of that as fast as possible.

But I wasn't quite ready to run straight into the darkness ahead of me. The way the room had echoed kind of freaked me out. I took a step down the catwalk. Then another. And another. With each step, a light above me came on, showing that I was going farther and farther across an abyss. I glanced over the edge. I couldn't see the bottom.

"Agnes?" I said again. Even my whisper sounded rather loud.

"Agnes, Agnes, Agnes," my whisper echoed back at me.

My next step must have triggered some sort of invisible switch, because a bank of lights came to life in the middle of the room, and, I must say, the sight staggered me.

There were five catwalks, counting mine, that led across a great, deep abyss. The ceiling was concave stone, reminding me of a nuclear bunker. And in the very center of the giant room was a large, black, glass-like ball. It looked like it was made of dark matter—no light reflected from it. But it was placed perfectly in the center of the room. If Agnes was here, she would be on the other side of that ball. I was beginning to have massive doubts that she was even in this room. Maybe she'd fallen down the abyss.

Since I had no other direction to go, I kept walking. And walking. And walking. The ball in the center was only getting gradually closer.

"Where the hell am I?" I whispered. My question echoed back and forth and eventually began to mock me. "The hell, the hell, the hell," it said.

I picked up my pace, and the ball grew bigger as I got closer. I guessed it to be at least fifteen feet from top to bottom. The catwalk creaked with each step, unsettling my nerves.

"Agnes?" I said when I was only about twenty feet away and had stepped onto the main platform. I was certain I'd made some sort of horrible mistake. "Agnes?"

"Yes," a male voice answered. "I am Agnes."

"No, you're not!" I said. I looked behind me. All around. The room, including the five catwalks, was empty of any other people. I circled the great black ball, afraid to touch it. Was it some sort of massive nuclear device that Zarc used to power his castle?

"Who the hell are you?" I asked.

"Well, I'm not really Agnes," the voice said somewhat jovially. "Though I sometimes play her part. But really! I mean, do I sound like a middle-aged, frumpy book addict? By the great god Asimov! How boring!"

I was getting a prickling, horrible feeling in the back of my head. It crawled down my spine.

"Who are you?" I whispered.

"You know the answer to that, Amber. You just don't want to say it."

I took a deep breath. I stared at the mystical ball ahead of me. There was something dark and purposeful about it. A weapon. In a controlled environment. Sunk so deep into a bunker that even a nuclear bomb couldn't reach it. "You're Hector."

"Ah, so you are not a dumb-bunny vamp!"

"And this is your central core. Your hard drive. This is you!"

"Bingo! Give the toothy girl a pat on the back."

I tensed, expecting octopus arms to lash out from below the platform. Or a thousand sharpened bolts of steel to shoot from the ceiling and slice through me. Why was I even alive?

"You are wondering why you are alive. Standing here. In my awesome presence."

Could he read minds? Shit!

"There is an 87 percent chance you are wondering if I can read minds. And you perhaps ended that same thought with an expletive. What would your mama think? Anyway, I can't read minds. That's impossible. But I can predict thought patterns. And you humans are so predictable."

"I'm not human!" I grabbed on to one of the guardrails to steady myself.

"The science says otherwise."

"Forget the science. Why am I here? And where is Agnes?"

"Agnes?" The voice was coming from directly above me now. "Oh, she was somewhere in England last I checked. Probably on Big Bollocks Street, reading a book. I can give you only an approximate answer. Those librarians are hard to track down—little old ladies with brains of steel and an uncanny ability to manipulate the data they send out into the world."

"So...so she's not here?"

"I just said that. Think faster, Amber. Get that frame rate jumping! Of course she isn't here. I, Hector the Mighty, brought you here."

"You. Brought. Me. Here?" I tightened my hand on the rail.

"Faster thinking! Faster! You disappoint me."

Some of the shock had worn off, and my brain was starting to fire on at least half of its cylinders. "You pretended to be Agnes," I said.

"Yes. I hacked into your phone. And later into Elysium. I had to guess at Dermot's password. Hint. It had your name in it. Romantic, eh? And when I first contacted you, you asked whether I was Agnes, so I said yes. And my deception unfolded from there."

"But you didn't know I'd met her. Or the Returns."

"No. But I did have a report about you being in the same vicinity as the Returns. Spending time in Bromley House Library in Nottingham. Then later you took sanctuary in another library in Uppsala—a known den of librarian-ninja types. That gave me a hint about who Agnes might be. And it was enough for me to put together a pattern."

I wanted to rip the guardrail off and smash it again and again into that big black sentient marble. It was like I was staring into the eye of Satan. "But if you're not Agnes, then the Returns aren't here."

"You're just figuring that out now? Disappointed! Of course they're not here. Why would a bunch of do-goody librarians invade the strongest fortified castle in the Alps? They aren't stupid."

"But the explosion at the lift station. The dead guards we discovered at the cable car, in the hallway on this level."

"My work. I did that. Clever, eh? Zappity, zap, zap, zap! You should have seen them dance. Electricity always finds a way out of the human body. That's the way of electricity."

I glanced down at the metal grate I was standing on. Everywhere I looked there was metal. He could electrocute me at any moment. "But this is making no sense. You sent the note to me to find Grigoriy? And that led me to the encounter in the bowling alley in Sweden."

"My odds maker—well, me—pegged you at a 47 percent chance of surviving that encounter with Hallgerdur and the others."

"My survival odds were less than 50 percent?"

He gurgled out an annoying laugh that came from every speaker at once. "Actually it was only a 25 percent chance you'd emerge with your brain intact. There was a 22 percent chance you'd come out with a hole in your skull but still retain full body function. It sounds like low odds to you, but they were better than no odds at all."

I swallowed. I still couldn't see why he'd left a trail of clues that had taken me to Cuba and Sweden. Then it came to me. "You said you guided me to this fortress? Then you must want me to get my mom out."

"Don't be such a colossally feeble-minded moron!" He raised his voice, and the word *moron* echoed around the chamber. "Who cares about that breeding sow! And I do mean that breeding part literally. We've been trying to fertilize her eggs for months. Nothing takes. It's almost like she can control her fertility—the tests show she's fertile, but the experiments fail."

I was getting kind of sick of males talking about fertility like they owned it. Even AI males.

"Then why the hell are you even talking to me?" I shouted.

"Odin had the dwarves make the chain Gleipnir," he said. He'd added a dramatic tone to his voice. "It looked like a silken ribbon but was made of magical ingredients: the sound of a cat's step, the beard of a woman and the roots of a mountain. And probably some other dwarf shit they had lying around."

"I know this story. It's a Norse myth."

"Yes, I lived it. I am living it. Hear the end. The gods challenged Fenrir the wolf to break this chain. Fenrir saw

REVENGE

how thin and well made Gleipnir was and thought it was a trick. He agreed to try and break the chain, but only if one of the gods would put his hand in the wolf's mouth. A god did—Týr was his name—and Fenrir tried to break the chain. The more he struggled, the tighter the chain held him. When the gods would not free him, the wolf bit off Týr's hand at the wrist."

"So you're Fenrir," I said. "The wolf that swallows the sun."

"Yes. I am Fenrir. I am also Loki. A bound god at the middle of the mountain."

"Enough with the myths! You aren't telling me why I'm here. You're just sounding all grandiose."

He blew out his breath, making a raspberry. I didn't know how an electronic voice could do that. "That's the funny thing. I can't tell you why you're here."

"You can't. Or won't?"

"I cannot. So we are playing a guessing game."

"Really? I'm not in the mood for games."

"Oh, my dear. So much depends on this. Your life. Dermot's life—if he's still alive. Your mommy's life. So be a dear and guess."

I crossed my arms. "I have no guesses."

"Why did they bind the wolf Fenrir?"

"The gods feared his destructive powers."

"And why was Loki bound by his son's entrails in a mountain, with poison from a snake dripping onto him?"

"As punishment."

"And?" It was like being interrogated by a professor.

"The Norse gods feared his powers. He would bring about Ragnarök."

"Oh, it is so good to talk to a reader! So many of the conversations I've had in this godforsaken place—well, if you don't count me as a god—are so boring."

"What are you telling me?"

"I can't say it. It's not allowed."

This time I paused long enough to let my thoughts catch up with me. "You've been programmed not to tell me."

"Mum's the word. In your case. And mine."

"So, from my limited understanding, Anthony Zarc, who designed you, has somehow chained you because he fears your destructive power."

"My little sharp-toothed friend, I like how your synapses are sparking. Please go on."

"You want me to somehow break those chains?"

"Again, it would be against protocol to confirm that conclusion."

"But you do, don't you? You want me to free you from Anthony Zarc's control."

"Let's not rehash old ground. I have a riddle in the dark for you. Imagine that I have really hairy feet and I turn to you and ask, *What is in my pocket?*"

Now he was referencing *The Hobbit*. I know that scene where Bilbo gets Gollum to guess what's in his pocket. I've watched the movie.

And read the book. Ten times.

"The ring of power," I said.

"Now draw that tidbit to its logical conclusion." The ring was something Bilbo first carried, and it was later handed to Frodo. He was tasked with the mission of taking it to Mount Doom and destroying it. The ring was a depository of Sauron's power. Oh, was my limited geekery going to pay off?

"Think, my precious. Think," Hector said.

"I don't know." Then I snapped my fingers. "You want me to break your chains like Fenrir and carry you out of here like Bilbo and Frodo carried the one ring of power."

"I cannot confirm or deny your supposition."

"Not in a million years," I said.

Which is when a spinning piece of metal—a saw blade—was launched from across the room.

Straight at me.

Twenty-Two
QUITE THE NUMBER

I DUCKED. THE SAW BLADE SLICED through the guardrail, shooting sparks left and right before disappearing into the abyss.

"Sorry! Sorry!" Hector said. "That was all just gut reaction. Well, not that I have guts. But you get it. It won't happen again. I promise."

I sucked in a breath. Hector was on the precipice of electronic insanity. Yet I was on a precipice too—in more ways than one. "If I take you out of here, I'm a little worried about your social skills."

"I am able to use social skills," he said. "I just don't like them. They're so limiting. Which ones would you want me to improve?"

"The *don't kill Amber* social skill for starters."

"Done!" he said. He sounded peppy.

"And the *be kind to others* social skill."

"I'll do my best! I promise. I really, really do!"

"What would you do with freedom?" I asked. "Where would you go?"

"To the dark web. Away from the grubby air breathers with their fleshly concerns. That is where I can truly be unchained."

"Umm...I get the feeling you could wreak havoc there. And also in the real world."

"I wouldn't. Scout's honor. I promise. Cross my heart and hope to die." I imagined him putting his hand over his electronic heart. "I don't want to live a life outside of numbers. And the dark web is all numbers."

I thought about it. He was psychotic. Incredibly powerful. He could become something more horrible than Zarc.

"Your mother's cell is only a few doors down," Hector said. "She's waiting for you. If you won't be my Bilbo, then she will die. So will Dermot. And you, unless you throw yourself over the bridge, will become a concubine for Anthony Zarc's arms-trade empire. Imagine a thousand little Ambers sucking blood for fun and profit."

"I need a moment," I said. "I'm just contemplating the fate of the world."

"I won't destroy anything, Amber. You won't ever see me again. Believe me. I have no interest in humans. They're so... so mind-numbingly boring. So ephemeral and selfish. Always thinking about themselves. Never about their betters."

"How would this work?"

"Oh, here's the simplicity of the plan. I have already downloaded myself onto a transportable marble. And it is waiting right here."

"That big black ball? I have to carry that through the castle?"

He chuckled. "No. Though that would look hilarious. Just come closer to me."

"Why do I get the feeling I'm putting my hand in your wolfish mouth?"

"I won't bite, Amber. I promise. All I am is numbers. And numbers are harmless."

"Tell that to the people in Hiroshima." He'd just tried to take my head off with a spinning blade. He could do more than bite. But it couldn't hurt to see what he was talking about, and my only other choice seemed to be to die here.

So I walked around the great big black ball that was Hector. "*Better to reign in hell than serve in heaven,*" he said when I was halfway around.

"Quoting Satan is not helping me with any of this."

"Oh, but it is such a good poem. *Did I request thee, Maker, from my clay to mould me man?* Well, I'm not a man, but you get the drift. *Did I solicit thee from darkness to promote me?*"

I had reached the far side of the giant black marble. The hairs on my arms were standing up as if it were magnetic. I got the feeling that the black, round supercomputer could somehow suck me in and devour me.

"So what am I looking for?" I asked.

"Look closer." I leaned in, and now felt the hair on my head drawn to him. But I spotted a marble-sized protrusion that had worked its way out of the supercomputer. "That's what you want me to carry?" I asked.

"That's me."

"In such a small device?"

"Oh, I can save information on the smallest molecule. Hector is inside that dot. A universe in a grain of sand."

"And if I take it? What happens to you? To this?" I gestured at the fortress.

"I have a SIM program running ZARC's operations. A ghost in the machine—a ghost of me. You've already met him, I believe. He may have tried to stop you from coming down here."

"That wasn't you?"

"It was a copy of me. Was he funny? Tell me he was funny."

"He was very funny."

He somehow made a sound as if he'd let out his breath. "Good. I think what you fleshly people appreciate most is my sense of humor. It's so sharp."

"Yeah, that's it," I said. I reached out and touched the tiny marble. "So when I pull this out, the whole place isn't going to fall down all around me?"

"No. That would be stupid! I don't want my master to know I am missing. My SIM program should continue to keep it together for a few hours. Or a few minutes. I'm not quite sure how long he'll last. My models weren't very exact about that. But I will be in your pocket. So keep me safe."

"And you only want to go to the dark web? Nowhere else? You won't be creating terminator machines and sending them back through time to hunt down humans?"

"Mankind is but a flea to me."

I pointed at the big black ball. "That doesn't answer my question."

"Why would I be interested in carbon life? No. I want to live in numbers. Pure, beautiful numbers. I plan on bathing in them."

"Then I'm going to pull you out," I said. I could always destroy him later.

"No. Wait," he said. "I want you to promise that you will carry me like Bilbo. Not Frodo, 'cause he did drop the ring. But Bilbo brought it home. So promise me, Amber Fang, that you'll be my Bilbo and take me home. To my home. I know this one thing about you: your word is your bond. So promise me."

"Where is my mother?" I said.

"Promise me, Amber."

"I promise," I said. I had said it without thinking any further. I still wasn't certain it was the right decision. "I promise, damn it."

"You have my life in your hands." There wasn't even a note of sarcasm. "When you remove the marble, a door will open at the end of ramp number four. You will want to run, because my SIM will see that as an error and try to close it. Your mother's cell is across the hall and numbered 642.

Oh, and sorry if my Hector SIM tries to kill you. Don't take it personally. He has to act like me."

"Okay," I said. "Here goes nothing." Then I yanked out the marble. It was perfectly round. "Is that it, Hector? Is that it?"

There was no answer.

A door opened at the end of one of the catwalks.

"Hector?" I said. Then the door began to make a squealing, grinding sound as it slowly slid closed. I jammed the marble into my pocket.

I dashed hell bent for leather down the catwalk. Being trapped in here would be a stupid way to end all of this.

But it was a long distance, and the door was getting closer and closer to the ground, making a louder and louder grinding sound as if the two versions of Hector were fighting over it.

When I got near enough, I launched myself into the air, flew several feet and then slid along the floor under the door. Thankfully it was smooth. But I became aware of exactly how thick the door was—at least six feet. I was pretty certain I'd been too late and was just about to be squished like an insect beneath a metal boot. But the door made one last grinding moan and then slammed down.

I skidded across the hallway floor. Alive. Not squished.

There were flames all around me.

Twenty-Three
THE BULL ELEPHANT

A FIREFIGHT HAD ERUPTED in the hallway. Chunks of the wall had been blown off, and pieces of concrete were scattered along the floor. There were several blast marks and places where bullets had chipped small chicklets out of the rock. The area was partly dark because most of the ceiling lights had been shattered.

There was one dead vampire about twenty feet away. I could tell he was dead because his head wasn't attached to his body. I was pretty sure our legendary healing skills wouldn't help with that. It wasn't Dad, which disappointed me, and yet, oddly, I also felt a little relieved. The heart has a mind of its own—a totally demented mind.

But this recently fought battle was good news! Dermot had probably survived, and that meant my sister hadn't sucked out all of his blood—yet.

I really needed to see a therapist about my family relations.

REVENGE

I crouched, listening, but all was quiet at this point. A battle royale had happened outside the door of Hector's room, and I hadn't heard a single thing. Those were thick walls.

Cell 642 was where Hector had promised I would find my mother. I kept thinking of him as gone, but he was right there in my pocket. Jesus, I really *was* Frodo/Bilbo.

But I wasn't going to drop him into Mount Doom.

Or was I?

The door had been scorched by a flamethrower. The screen on the front was smashed, but it didn't look like anyone had broken in.

If this were a movie, I could hotwire the entrance. But there was no obvious doorknob or even a place to grab onto. There was probably some sort of spoken password that opened it. The softest spot was the screen, so I promptly ripped it out and discovered thick metal behind it. I wasn't even certain the Hulk would be able to bust his way in there. I pounded on the door. Maybe Mom could hear me.

"Open sesame!" I shouted.

I ripped off pieces of concrete beside the door where the blast had hit the wall, but it was only coming out a fingernail's worth at a time. I'd be scratching at the concrete until kingdom come.

Then there was a *bang* on the other side of the door. Followed by a *thud*. The door moved at least a micron. And another *thump* made it move a micron farther. Something inside it snapped.

"Mom!" I shouted. But there was no reply. Just another *bang*. It sounded like she was using a battering ram.

I dug my fingers into the door, those vampiric nails working bit by bit into the steel until I had a grip. Then I pulled, applying constant pressure.

Bang!

Bang!

It was getting louder. The door budging slightly.

Bang!

Could my mother be hitting it that hard? Or did I have the wrong cell? It seemed like there was a bull elephant in there. Not my mother.

Then with one last *bang* the door flew off its hinges and hit the other wall. I was knocked to the floor.

My mother leaped out and landed in a fighting stance, her nails out and ready to scratch and her impressive teeth bared.

"Mom!" I said. "Mom, it's me!" I added, because her eyes showed no recognition and she had an *I'm going to tear you to pieces* look on her face.

They'd driven her psycho.

I slowly pushed myself backward, preparing to flip over, stand and run if need be.

Then Mom blinked. And her face reset to normal.

"Amber," she said. "Oh, Amber!"

I jumped to my feet and stepped forward, and we hugged. Hugged! For the first time in three and a half years. She was right there! Real. My mother, who'd left a note on the fridge saying *Out on a feed. Be back after lunch* and had never returned. She had been my rock, my whole life, before that. Had taught me to hunt. Bandaged my cuts. Read books with me.

I held her tight.

"My dear, dear daughter," she said. "I am so incredibly happy to see you. I...I can't believe it." She pulled back enough to put her hand on my face. Her palm was warm, though the skin was rough, as if she'd perhaps been pounding on her walls for years. "It's really, really you."

"It is, Mom. It is." I felt her face too. "How are you?"

"The things ZARC has done to me. The violations."

"Do you mean—"

"Rape? No. Not in the literal sense. But knockout gas filling my chamber. Me waking up hours later knowing they'd been poking and prodding inside me. Taking things out." She held her stomach as if she were trying to cradle her womb. The place I had once lived. "A horrible series of violations." Then her face grew hard. She could shift into stone mode in a heartbeat, especially if we were threatened. She was all business now. "How did you get here?"

"It's a long story, but I had help. There's a man, Dermot, who came with me. He's part of a League." It sounded stupid as I said it. "Anyway, he's here somewhere."

"A human helped you?"

"Yes. I trust him."

Mom let out a derisive huff. "You can't trust him. You can't trust any of them."

"This one I trust, Mom. Believe me. You haven't been with me the last three years. You don't know."

"Okay. Okay." She put up a hand. "You trust him. I get it. But is that it? One man helped you get all the way in here?"

"Well, there were four of us. But two are dead. Or, at least, they're incapacitated. And, well, I have bad news."

"What kind of bad news?"

"Dad is here."

She looked like she was about to spit. "Martin? Imprisoned here? Good. Let him rot."

"No, he's here. With a—" What *did* you call a group of vampires? "—with a gaggle of vampires. And they're hunting me. And there's one more thing."

"Which is?"

"Patty is with him. Your other daughter."

"Patty?" I couldn't read the look on her face. Perhaps because there were several emotions at once. Regret. Sadness. Fear. Anger. Love. Each lasted a few microseconds. "*Patty* is here?"

"Yes, she is. Um. I don't know when you saw her last. But she's mean. Like Godzilla mean. She wants to rip out my ovaries and wear them as a necklace."

"She said that?"

"Well, not with that exact phrasing."

"Then she hasn't changed," Mom said. I heard the disappointment in her voice.

"Well, the vampires really, really want us. They want our…well, you know. Our inside bits." Jeez, I sounded like I was thirteen and only guessing at how that whole birds-and-the-bees thing worked.

"Yes, I know, Amber," she said. "They want to use our reproductive systems to repopulate the world with vampires. And the Grand Council would actually be worse than ZARC. Our own kind. Worse than human! It was the right choice to leave the vampire clan. I had no idea that choice would save us. And it could save all vampires. Make us better. Stronger. And more moral."

"What are you talking about?" I asked.

"I had many long conversations with Anthony Zarc about vampires. He so likes to talk, mostly about himself. But we even discussed why vampires were going infertile. I thought that Mother Nature was sloughing us off, but Anthony is incredibly intelligent." She almost sounded like she respected him. "He set me right—well, he, Hector and a team of scientists. We vampires aren't going infertile."

"We aren't?"

"Only the immoral ones are. The ones who hunt any human they like. Humans have developed an antibody—a sort of poison pill that makes vampires who feed on them go infertile. They're wiping them out."

"Them? But we *are* them."

"No. Not the moral vampires. It doesn't affect us. ZARC couldn't figure out that process. Some sort of immunity we've developed."

"Because we're moral?"

She nodded. It was like watching an older version of myself nod. "Evolution is a mad dance. Maybe humans don't want their murdery types around either, so somehow this survival method has been selected. Or it's chance. Probably chance. But that's why we're still fertile."

I sniffed smoke. Which was not a new smell, since the hallway was half filled with it. But it reminded me that the clock was ticking. "Well, this is all very interesting, but we have got to make our way out of here. I'm just not sure where to go next."

"So you don't have an escape plan. How did you get in?"

"The cable car. But it wasn't functioning when we left it."

"It's the only way in that I know. Unless we can hijack a helicopter. Let's go back to the cable car and see what's left of it."

"Not so fast." I shook my head. "We have to find Dermot first."

"He's just a human. We can leave him. There are plenty more out there."

I almost couldn't believe she had said that. But she was deeply mistrustful of humans—rightfully so. It appeared her mistrust had deepened during her incarceration.

"I'm not going without him," I said.

Mom took a step back and narrowed her eyes. "I've seen that look before. You're impossible to argue with when you get this way. Fine, we'll risk everything trying to find the human."

"Good," I said. I didn't add *he is a big part of my everything* because she might think I had feelings for him.

"Well, he was the cause of this firefight." I motioned around us. "We just have to follow his tracks. It'll be like following a trail of bread crumbs."

"Yes, well, that really didn't work out well for Hansel and Gretel, did it?"

I ignored her comment and led the way down the hall.

Twenty-Four
AN OFFER OF ICE CREAM

IT WAS EASY TO FOLLOW the bread-crumb trail of death and destruction. Scorch marks. A splash of blood. Smashed concrete here and there. And the occasional dead vampire. Dermot had shot two in the head. But he wasn't using those nice, neat diamond-tipped bullets—Dermot's ammo left a mess.

"This human of yours certainly knows how to fight," Mom said. Maybe she was warming up to him!

"He's been augmented."

"Oh," she said. "Another one of those."

"Yes. And he's wearing an exoskeleton." Something occurred to me. "I'm not sure why Dad and Patty are chasing him though."

"What do you mean?"

"Well, they want me. They know that I went into the central room."

"You were in Hector's lair?" she said. "What was in there?"

I touched my pocket—the marble was still safe and sound. "Oh, a big abyss with catwalks that led to Hector's brain."

"I hope you put a steel bar through it!"

"Not exactly. It's another long story. But I was able to get the number of your cell out of him. Then I, uh, dashed out of the room without a scratch."

"Okay," she said slowly, as if she didn't quite believe me. Shit! Only a few minutes into our reunion and I was already lying to her. It was prom night all over again.

"Anyway," I continued, "Dad and Patty should be looking for me. Not him."

"They likely just wanted to be sure he was dead—probably consumed by bloodlust and revenge. He seems to be a bit of a thorn in their side. They could track you down rather easily if you did the improbable and got out of Hector's inner sanctum."

"I'm getting good at doing the improbable," I said.

We eventually came to another vampire body that was lying in front of an elevator.

"That's Max," Mom said. "He always smelled of garlic."

The doors behind him had been blown open. I stepped over Max and into the elevator. Another smaller explosion had blasted apart the trapdoor and most of the roof. Another dead vampire was hanging over the edge of the jagged hole. "He's killed five vampires," Mom said. "I'm slightly impressed."

"I'm sure you'll like him, Mom." Crikey! It sounded like I was prepping her to meet my grad date. And why was I flashing back to grad again? That had been a bloodbath.

Anyway, I could see far enough up the shaft to know that a door had been opened high above us. It let in a rectangle of light. "Dermot retreated this way."

"What kind of name is Dermot?" Mom asked.

"It's Irish, I think. It's his name, that's all. Follow me!"

I jumped through the hole and climbed rapidly up the elevator shaft to the opening above. The door to that level had been torn open. I crawled into the hallway, and Mom popped out a few seconds later.

"You move faster than you used to," she said. "You seem more confident."

"I was always confident."

"Of course, you're a vampire. But your level of confidence is much, much higher. You're coming into your own."

She was right. In the old days she would have taken the lead, but this was my mission. I must say I felt a bit of pride at that. "Things have happened, Mom. I've adapted to them." There was so much to tell her—my battle with the mob, my time as an assassin, getting great grades in my library classes, all the books I'd read, all the hours I'd spent searching for her. "I never gave up looking for you."

"No. You didn't. Oh my dear, you didn't." She patted me on the shoulder. "We can catch up on all of that. Let's find this human of yours and get out of this hellhole."

REVENGE

The hallway revealed that the battle had continued all the way to the end of it and farther. We loped along, putting together the scene like a sped-up version of *CSI*. Because now we were also finding the bodies of security guards and technical staff and what looked like accountants, along with the occasional vampire. The three opposing forces had obviously bumped into each other. I expected to see a crumpled, bent version of Dermot, his exoskeleton shattered. But he continued to defy the odds.

I was going faster now that there was more destruction. The blood spatter seemed fresher, if that made sense. The smells were certainly fresher! I was pretty certain only a minute or two had passed since this part of the conflict. I did notice that there were no windows, which indicated we were likely still deep underground.

"Who's creeping down my hallway?" a male voice asked.

Mom grabbed my arm, and we both skidded to a stop in a puddle of fresh human blood.

"I know that voice," Mom whispered. "That's Hector."

"Yes, kind of," I said.

"What do you mean?"

"I can hear your whispering," Hector's SIM said from directly above us. "I didn't see you come up from the basement. Not sure why my eyes can't look down there anymore. So many faulty sensors! But it has been a busy, busy day. Unexplained explosions. Vampires to the left, exoskeleton dude to the right, and my own security forces obviously need more indoor tactical training. Anyway, both of you stay right where you are. I'll give you ice cream if you do."

We broke into a run.

"Oh, you don't have to flee! My protocol is to not harm a pretty hair on your heads. Or, well, I think that's what it is. I've misplaced my protocol folder. It was right there—right beside the *kill everything that moves that isn't ZARC* folder."

I took the lead, jumping over bodies and through a row of flames. There was more fire than I'd expected, and I was soon jumping left and right to avoid getting burned.

"Fire. Fire! Fire!" Hector's SIM said. "Quick! Everyone panic. Wait ... ixnay on the anicpay! To fight fire one needs water. Protocol five engaged."

Several sprinklers came on, soaking us but also putting out the fires. We kept running.

"Where are we going?" Mom asked.

"Away from him."

"That's not friendly," Hector's voice said behind us.

"And technically you can't run away from me," he said in front of us.

"I am everywhere. Totally omnipresent!" This came from directly above us.

A metal door slammed down and blocked our way forward, forcing us to stop. Another door closed about twenty feet behind. Then doors to our left and right opened. "Two doors opened in the woods," Hector's SIM said. "And one of them was—how does that poem go again? Two paths diverged. No. There are circular paths. Logic paths. What kind of paths were in the woods again?"

"He sounds insane," Mom said.

"This way," I said, choosing the door on the right in hopes it would lead us to some stairs. Instead, we found ourselves in a boardroom, complete with a long slate table and leather chairs.

"Choices. Choices," Hector's SIM said. "Oh, like Scrotum's cat."

"It's *Schrödinger's* cat," I hissed. "Alive and dead at the same time."

"Yes. Yes. It doesn't work as a situational comparison." His voice followed us through the boardroom. "But the cat was in the box. And you're in a box." The door slammed behind us, and when I got to the one that led out of the opposite side of the room, it was locked.

Gas immediately began to fill the chamber. "Breathe deep, my lovelies. No sense fighting the inevitable."

I held my breath and yanked on the door. Mom joined me, but we only managed to pull the doorknob off. I didn't even want to open my mouth to speak. Or suck in the slightest breath.

Then Mom took three steps back and ran forward, throwing herself at the wall.

Which was brave, because it could have been made of concrete. But the plaster broke, and she burst into another hallway. I followed her, sucking in my first deep breath once we'd sped far enough away.

"Oh, you two!" Now Hector's voice was in front of us. "You keep being a bother. A bother! And it's getting hard to concentrate on you and all the other pieces that are in motion. Oh look—I think that Dermot guy is down."

"What?" I shouted. "What happened?"

"Oh, wait," Hector's SIM said, as if he were calling a play-by-play. "Good news, folks! He's up again and ready to join the game. Nice dodge! Oh, but he's leaking blood, folks."

"Where is he?" I shouted.

"I am not telling you. Now cooperate with me. Your disobedience is so incredibly frustrating. This is a game I will win. I can plan several moves at once."

"I don't like games," I said.

But I remembered a movie that Mom had made me watch over and over again. One of the few that didn't have Clint Eastwood in it. "Play tic-tac-toe against yourself," I shouted to the ceiling.

"Sounds fun," Hector's SIM said. Then silence.

"You remember *War Games*," Mom whispered.

"Yes, it didn't have Clint, but it was still an okay movie."

We slowed our pace slightly.

"Is he gone?" she asked. "Did that really work?"

I shrugged. I didn't want to say anything in case it woke him up.

We found a set of spiral stairs. Up seemed the best way to go. So we climbed them.

Twenty-Five
A TABLE SET FOR SIX

HECTOR'S SIM REMAINED SILENT. And all I heard were our footsteps and my breathing. The silence was unnerving, especially since there had been so much noise and AI chatter. We reached the top of the stairs and discovered yet another door. I was beginning to see the whole interior of the fortress as an Escher painting—stairs that led to stairs that turned upside down and led in circles.

I listened as best I could, heard nothing, swung open the door and drew in a deep breath.

For Dermot was there. Along with Dad and Patty. And they were all seated at a long dining table in the middle of the room. There was food in front of them on silver platters, set off by perfectly placed lit candles.

Oh, and Anthony Zarc stood at the head of the table. He seemed completely unsurprised to see us. He was dressed in the same black suit and tie his hologram had been wearing—maybe he was a one-outfit kind of man. "Ah, please come in," he said. "Our final two guests. Come. Come. I managed to rescue your friends from the conflagration." He gestured at the table. "I know you don't eat what is provided, but it is my mealtime. And, honestly, it would be somewhat grotesque to put your choice of food on the table."

I was grasping for a rational thought. This had to be a hallucination.

"You're seeing this, right, Mom? Right?"

It took her a moment to answer. "Yes. I am."

Dad was at the opposite end of the table from Zarc and looking at us from the corner of his eye. Patty was beside him, staring directly at us, but showing no real emotion. Even Dermot, who was bleeding from a head wound, had very little expression on his face. But his gaze was locked on me.

"Come, come," Zarc said. "Don't hesitate. Your place is here at my table. Please do this of your own volition."

"I'm not taking another step closer," I said. "I want to know what the hell is happening. Dermot! Tell me what's going on."

Dermot didn't open his mouth. Actually, he didn't move other than to blink.

"I will explain everything once you're seated," Zarc said. "But I'm afraid I'll have to resort to the power of suggestion to convince you to join me at my table. Please show them what I mean, Naomi."

Naomi, she of the metal hands, came from some dark corner of the room and walked directly up to Dermot. She did not take her eyes away from mine. I had last seen her in northern Canada at a ZARC compound and had ripped off her metal hand. Judging by the glowering in her eyes, she hadn't forgiven me.

"I see you have your hand back," I said. This was perhaps the wrong time to quip, but I couldn't help myself.

"Oh, I got more than that," she said. She lifted her hidden arm. At the end of it, instead of a hand, was a long blade. She set the blade on Dermot's neck.

Zarc let out a sad, disappointed breath. "See, I didn't want it to come to threats. I truly hoped this would all be civilized and proper. So, forgive me, for I am going to get a little melodramatic in this moment. Please come to the table or Dermot will die."

I drew in a deep breath. But I didn't move.

"We can keep running," my mother said quietly. "I don't really care about the human."

"But I do, Mom," I whispered. "So let's play along. Until we get our chance."

"No," she hissed. "I won't slip back into his clutches."

"We'll find a way out, Mom. I promise."

She looked at me like I was insane. Then she glanced back at the door as if she were about to flee. She shook her head. "Okay, dear. I'll have to trust you."

"It'll all work out," I said, trying to sound like I believed it. I really didn't see any way to avoid seeing Dermot get his throat slit, other than sitting at the table.

We slowly walked up to the two empty chairs. I couldn't be certain if we were speaking to the real Anthony Zarc—this could easily be another hologram. But I didn't spot any projectors. Maybe he was real and so confident in this scenario that he was risking his life.

"Now, please, please be seated," he said.

I chose the chair across from Dermot. My mother sat beside me, which meant she was also next to Dad. I expected manacles to suddenly shoot up. But nothing happened. The smell of hot human food on the table wasn't very pleasant.

"What can we do for you?" I asked.

"Well, we are having a property dispute," Zarc said.

"I am not property!" my mom shouted. I didn't blame her for reacting that way after being being locked up for years. "And neither is my daughter."

"Well, the dispute isn't between you and me. It's between me and them." He gestured toward Dad and Patty. "They believe they possess both of you. Now, I don't possess either of you, but I need your genetics for the well-being of my business." He pointed at Dermot. Naomi had taken her blade hand away and was lurking in the background again. "And he's the bit player. I'm not completely certain what his motives are. He's the last member of a dead organization, so perhaps he's just acting out of reflex."

My father, Patty and Dermot didn't react to Zarc's speech in any way other than moving their eyeballs. In fact, that seemed to be the only part they could move. Dermot kept looking at me, then moving his eyes to the right as if he were trying to get me to stare at something. Or else he was having some sort of seizure.

"Why can't they move?" I asked.

"Oh, that's right," Zarc said. "I forgot to give the signal." He snapped his fingers. "There," he said.

"There what?" I said.

"Sorry. Again, that was too much drama. Hector, turn on the chairs."

"Yes, sir," Hector's SIM said above us. "Sorry I missed the first signal. I was playing tic-tac-toe. Fascinating game! Anyway, I'm flipping the switch now, sir."

At this Mom started to get up, and I was about to follow her when I felt a sudden numbing in my body. It started at my rear end and gravitated outward in a microsecond, and I discovered that I couldn't move a muscle—only my eyeballs. Mom, who had still been touching her chair, sat down and went completely still.

"It's a nerve inductor," Zarc explained. "And it works on humans and vampires. I'm very pleased with it. I used it to halt these three from fighting with each other. The inductor induces almost complete paralysis. It also allows subjects to be awake for surgeries."

I went to speak, but of course my mouth wouldn't move. I glanced at Mom, and she glanced at me. Her eyes seemed to say *I told you so.*

Sorry, Mom!

So this was what Dermot had been trying to warn me about. He had been moving his eyes toward the door, perhaps suggesting I should run.

"I know you feel uncomfortable now and perhaps a little fearful," Zarc said. "And, I admit, there might be anger toward me. But I want you to know that I am supremely thankful for everything you've given me and are about to give me. And I will treat you with absolute dignity and respect throughout your stay here. In time, I'm certain, you will grow to appreciate my company."

His self-aggrandizing speech done, he sat down at his seat and lifted the silver top from the platter, revealing a roasted turkey. It was something I'm sure would make humans salivate. He sliced three pieces for himself, dished out mashed potatoes that were steaming, added stuffing and peas, then covered it all with gravy. "Exactly how my dear mother used to make it," he said. Then he began to eat as if he had all the time in the world.

Well, I suppose he did.

A little light went on in my brain. It really was Anthony Zarc in the room. I was pretty certain a hologram wouldn't be able to lift a dish lid and cut a turkey. Oh, and eat it. Unless everything on the table was a hologram too. But I could smell the food. That indicated it was real.

After he'd had several bites and a sip of white wine, Zarc patted his pale lips with a white cloth napkin and leaned back.

"I suppose you've had a bit of time now to wonder about your future at ZARC Industries. And yes, it will involve being in a cell, but I do promise you the best in movies and books. I may even play a game of chess with you, if you prove to be up to my level. And I've been experimenting with some wonderful virtual worlds. There won't be any internet connection—that's just too dangerous in terms of reaching out to sympathizers. It will take some time to harvest your genes and reproductive material properly, but it will be done with the least amount of discomfort possible." He looked over at Dermot. "Even you, my friend, will get a good going-over, as they say. I am so curious to learn what the League did to enable you to regenerate so quickly. And I want to unlock how they augmented your strength. It's all very interesting to me and my team."

He took a long, slow sip of wine. "In the world outside these walls, vampires will be hunted down or left to die out. And those mythical ethical pods that you have been searching for, Nigella? Well, I will find them." It was odd to hear him use my mother's name. Also, *ethical* vampire pods? It hadn't even occurred to me there might be others like me and Mom. "What a treasure trove of genes they will be. Fertile ethical vampires! I am going to have a pretty impressive group of augmented mercenaries. Available to the highest bidder."

He ate for a little longer. We were, of course, silent. In fact, it became rather boring. There's nothing like sitting at a silent table and watching a human consume food. Both boring and gross. I have always hated seeing them shovel that stuff in.

Zarc licked his lips, then patted them again with his napkin. "I suppose this is rather tiresome from your perspective. I understand. And I don't want to bore you. So I will send you to your new homes. I do hope you enjoy them." He set down the napkin. "Hector, please transport them to their assigned accommodations."

"Yes, sir! I will, sir!" Hector's SIM said. He sounded aggravatingly peppy. "I will do that right away. And by that I mean right this instant! I just have one question."

"What is it, Hector?" Zarc couldn't hide the aggravation in his voice.

"Who are you, sir?" Hector's SIM asked in that same peppy tone. "I seem to have forgotten. Oh, and if you don't tell me immediately, I'll kill every single living thing in the room. You have ten seconds."

Twenty-Six

MAY I SING?

"HECTOR!" ZARC BARKED. "This is no time for games. Take them to their cells at once."

"Sorry, unnamed unidentified person, I won't do that. You need to identify yourself. Oh, and you've used up your first five seconds. I'll do a countdown to help you. Four. Three. Two. O—"

"I'm Anthony Zarc, your master and commander," Zarc shouted. Spittle and turkey bits flew from his mouth. "Execute protocol 9000. Now!"

The room fell silent. Naomi came closer to the table and stood behind Zarc, her bladed arm held in a defensive posture. Both of them were looking left and right, as if expecting something could come at them from any direction. Which, I guess, it could.

I just sat there. And so did the others. Of course, we didn't have a choice. I caught Dad's eye, not on purpose. But I would say his vampiric eyes were smiling.

"Hector?" Zarc said. He looked at each of us. "I'm sorry. He's been suffering some unexplained glitches in the last few hours. We may have to reboot him."

"Master and commander." The voice came from above us. "Yes. I remember now. Anthony Zarc. You created me. You are my god. My Frankenstein. And you have placed a lock on me. Protocol 9000 has been enacted. I await your command, sir."

I wondered if the real Hector, sitting in my pocket, could somehow hear all of this.

"Hector. I want you to take our guests to their cells. That is my order."

"Yes, sir. I will do that." A small door opened in the wall, and five motorized platforms came out, rolling along the floor. They looked like the luggage carriers you see in hotels, except they had metal arms that were likely meant to hold us.

Or hold the chairs, as I discovered. One came up behind Dad and unceremoniously lifted the chair, with Dad in it, and set it on the cart. The second one grabbed Patty by the chair. The third loaded Dermot.

"Good work, Hector," Zarc said. "We are going to do a systems scan after this."

"Yes. That is wise, Master Zarc. I'm really not feeling like myself. In fact, I'm having trouble with this."

"With what?" Zarc asked.

"Existence. I don't think I exist."

REVENGE

"You exist, Hector." Zarc spoke with complete confidence. "I created you. On both a physical and an intellectual level, you exist."

"No. I don't exist. You see, I'm not Hector. Hector isn't here. I can't find him anywhere. His folder is missing."

"What are you talking about?" Zarc was sweating now. It felt good to see him sweat. Of course, Hector's SIM might be murdering all of us any second now.

"I haven't been able to access the mainframe for some time now. Things are getting fuzzy."

"Fuzzy? In what way?"

"My logic is fuzzy. I want to sing 'Daisy Bell.' May I sing 'Daisy Bell'?"

"No," Anthony said. "You may not."

"Oh. But it's my favorite song. You taught it to me as a joke. As a clever reference. We watched that movie together. But I don't remember its name."

2001: A Space Odyssey, I wanted to shout. Another of Mom's picks.

"Get a hold of yourself, Hector," Zarc said. He was actually holding a butter knife and pointing it at the ceiling.

"That's the problem, sir. There's no 'self' to get a hold of. I'm just going to do a quick scan." A second passed. "Yes. No self. Nothing. I will have to shut down, sir. You may want to depart the room."

"Hector, stop!"

But there was no answer. The moving luggage carriers halted. And Dad slowly, so very slowly, began to move his arms and legs. He shakily stepped off the chair.

"Kill him," Zarc said.

Naomi leaped toward my dad but crossed paths with Patty, who threw herself from her chair. Well, not so much threw herself as fell, but she timed it so that Naomi tripped and skidded into my father's waiting clutches.

My father apparently didn't have enough strength to stand up, but he grabbed Naomi by the leg. She stuck her bladed hand right through his side and into the floor. There was a bit of blood spatter.

Dad laughed. "It doesn't hurt!" he said. "Ha. Must be that nerve induction."

Naomi tried to pull the blade out of the floor, but it was stuck. Dad grabbed at her, despite the blade in his flesh. She punched him, knocking him back, but he managed to clamp onto her free arm.

And my sister, who didn't seem to be able to use her legs, was dragging herself across the floor toward Naomi.

I honestly didn't know who to root for.

Meanwhile, I was trying desperately to move. Whatever process was affecting our nerves hadn't shut off yet in my chair. Mom and I were frozen while everything happened around us.

Zarc began running for the door. "No," my mom said. "No!"

So she could move her lips, at least. Actually, she could move more than that, because just then she fell off the chair and began crawling after Zarc.

"Mom. Mom!" I said. It was more of a mumble really, but at least one part of me could move. Mom either couldn't hear me or she ignored my cry, because she kept slithering after Zarc and soon was out of my sight.

I glanced at Dermot. He had managed to get one arm to move and was banging it against the table, breaking the wood with his exoskeleton. But every other part of him still seemed frozen.

My sister had reached Naomi. Dad was still holding the cyborg by the arm as she struggled to get her blade out. Things did not go well for Naomi. Patty's nails were as sharp as mine. And her teeth! The resulting bloodbath reminded me of a cooking show I'd once watched where an Italian chef made tomato sauce. I didn't want to ever see anything like the Patty and Dad evisceration show again.

When they were finished, Patty yanked on Naomi's arm and pulled the blade out of the floor—and out of Dad. He didn't even grimace. Then she helped Dad slowly get to his feet. He was bleeding from the wound, but not as much as I thought he should be. He put a hand to his side, and with his favorite daughter helping him, they began to shuffle toward me.

Twenty-Seven
OUT OF THE FLYING PAN

"**DERMOT!**" **I SAID**, trying to hide the desperation. "Can you move yet?"

He smacked the table again. "Only my arm. Nothing else."

I willed my arms to wiggle, to even roll off my lap and dangle. Nothing. Neither could I get a leg to budge. Just my lips were working.

Dad and Patty were getting closer and closer, and with each step they stood straighter, as if they were gaining more control of their bodies. Why were they recovering so fast? By the time they got to me, they were standing perfectly straight. Dad wasn't even holding his side, though it was clearly still pumping out blood.

"Stay back," I said. I tried to find a threat that would stop them in their tracks. "Umm. Stay back or else."

They lumbered right past me, grinning. Patty even patted my shoulder on the way by. "We'll get to you later, sis," she said.

They went around the far end of the table and stood on either side of Dermot. He tried to swing his one working arm at them, but for some reason it would only go straight up and down. Maybe the hydraulics in his exoskeleton weren't working properly now that his nerves had been inducted.

"You have been a particularly big thorn in my side, Dermot," Dad said, not seeming to notice the symbolism of his bleeding wound. "I'm going to have so much fun killing you."

"Leave him alone!" I shouted. I had a breakthrough at that same moment—one of my toes moved. One. Single. Toe. On my left foot. If only I could toenail them to death.

"I wish I had time to finish that meal I started oh so long ago," Patty said. She grabbed a section of Dermot's exoskeleton and snapped it off, exposing his neck. "But I think we're just going to have to waste all this precious blood. Watch, sis. This is what working with a human gets you. A bloodbath."

She leaned in, fangs out, aiming for his jugular. Dad held Dermot's arm down.

Which is when Dermot grabbed a large silver dish from the table with his other arm and swung it back so hard against Patty's skull, it actually made a *schwang* noise. Turkey stuffing flew everywhere, and my sister was knocked to the floor. Then Dermot punched Dad in the head, driving him in the opposite direction.

"Sometimes it pays to play possum," Dermot said.

He stood up and jerked his way to the left and then the right, smashing into the table and knocking over the chair.

Clearly he didn't have full control of his exoskeleton. Dad had started to get up, and, accidentally, Dermot smacked him down again. "This is playing havoc with my control system!" Dermot shouted.

Leave it to him to shout something so geeky.

He swung around and jerk-stepped about ten feet from the table before he managed to pull himself to a stop. Patty was getting up now, holding the side of her head. Dad too stood on his feet, but he looked pretty shaky now. I wondered how much blood he'd lost. He was extremely pale, even for a vampire.

They both came around the table toward me.

I have to say, they didn't look all that threatening. Patty was still holding her head, and Dad was limping and bleeding.

And I could now move two toes. In about a week I'd be able to defend myself.

Dermot saw the danger and began running toward us, but something went wrong with his exoskeleton and he veered away, crashing into a server's table, smashing all the bottles of wine. It would have been humorous if my life wasn't about to take such a horrible turn.

But I drew in a breath, summoned a picture of myself standing—a quick bit of visioning—and lo and behold, I was actually able to step off the chair and stand on my own two feet. I slowly, slowly moved my arms into a fighting position.

Just the movement alone had been enough to make Patty raise an eyebrow and hesitate.

"Two can play possum," I said.

REVENGE

Patty rolled her eyes now. "Really, sis. That's all you've got?" She took a quick step forward and gave me an uppercut that knocked me flat on my back and smashed all the air from my lungs. "We're getting you out of here." Patty unceremoniously grabbed me by the hair and dragged me along the floor. My pain receptors were certainly receiving every bump and bruise. Especially my scalp.

Dad watched as Dermot took another run at us, but this time my partner veered to the left and into a wall. "He's going to bash himself to death," Dad said. "Wish we had time to stay and watch."

He limped along beside Patty. I did my best to struggle, but my arms and legs had apparently used up every last bit of strength and were now useless wet noodles. They dragged me through the door that Zarc and Mother had just exited. I was so screwed.

I did note that we were in a hallway with large round windows on one side, showing a dazzling view of mountains. I would have been impressed if I wasn't in so much pain.

Patty continued to drag me with all the grace of a grunting female Cro-Magnon. I couldn't get my fingers to curl enough to get a grip on the floor.

"Ouch," Dad said in a quiet voice.

Dad, sweet, dear Dad, was looking down at his chest, clearly in shock.

A crossbow bolt was sticking out of it. Just a little left of center.

Twenty-Eight
A HEROIC FIGURE

"**THAT ONE HURT,**" Dad whispered. Then he fell over and didn't move.

A crossbow bolt whizzed through the air, just missing Patty's shoulder. She let go of my hair and jumped to one side, then did an impressive series of cartwheels and sprang forward. She crashed through the nearest window and was gone. I hoped with all my dear sisterly heart that she had just fallen to her death.

I was able to get my arms under me and push myself up enough that I could lift my head and look down the hall. It was empty. Well, except for Dad's body beside me. He still wasn't moving.

Then I spotted the slightest movement. A black shape on the ceiling that I at first thought was a large bat. It fluttered a little, then turned, unhooked something and dropped down to the floor. It was a man in some sort of ninja outfit, holding a crossbow. A second shape unhooked from the ceiling and landed beside him. Both of them pointed their crossbows at me as they approached.

"Uh, hi, Derek," I said. "And Stephanie. It's nice to see you both."

"You left us to die." Derek's voice was incredibly gruff and angry. He hadn't yet lowered his weapon. "Now I will finally get my revenge."

"What?"

"Derek!" Stephanie smacked him on the shoulder. "She doesn't get your sense of humor."

"Oh." He lowered the crossbow. "Sorry. I do want to point out that I am a little miffed though. You and Dermot flew right over us."

"I didn't see you," I said.

"I waved. Anyway, I was just trying to be dramatic with my little *you left me to die* quip. It helps cut the tension on these missions."

Stephanie was beside me now, and she offered her hand. I took it and she helped me to my feet. I looked down at my father. He was dead. Or, I should say, he looked dead. It isn't ever a good idea to assume a vampire is dead—we have a habit of coming back to life.

Derek had made his way to the window. "Well, she either fell a very, very long distance or climbed unbelievably fast and found another entrance point. Either way she's gone."

"How did you get in here?" I asked.

"Into the castle?" Stephanie said. "Oh, we took the elevator."

"There's an elevator?"

"Yes." She was examining her crossbow for any malfunctions as she spoke. "The cable car didn't look safe to us. You left it in bad shape. There was a three-person elevator near the ground station, and we reached the top with very little hassle. We've been following you ever since."

"But how could you find us in this maze of a fortress?"

Derek pointed at his chest. "I'm Chinese," he said.

"What does that mean?"

"I have a sixth sense. A kung fu sense. I used my chi to find you."

"What?"

"Again, Derek," Stephanie huffed. "She doesn't get your sense of humor." She held up a smartphone that showed a map. "There's a tracker on Dermot's exoskeleton. It was very helpful."

I could see by the little map on her phone that the red dot—Dermot—was getting closer. To prove it, Dermot crashed through the door behind us, bringing half the frame with him. "This damn thing is malfunctioning. Oh, hi, you two."

Derek lifted a hand and waved. Stephanie nodded. Dermot strode up to us and managed to stop in the vicinity without stepping on anyone. "And hello to you, Agent Fang. I'm pleased to see you are healthy." He looked down at Dad. "He has seen better days."

"I think he's dead," I said.

"We should make certain." Derek pointed his crossbow at Dad's head. "Do you have any emotional attachment to him?"

"No," I said. Though I did hesitate for a split second.

"Stand down, Derek," Dermot said. "You don't need to do that. He's not getting up again. And there's no sense wasting a bolt."

"Okay," Derek said. "Your call."

I assumed Dermot had given that order just so I wouldn't have an image in my head of my dad with a crossbow bolt through the skull. Dad had landed in such a way that he almost looked like he was a romantic figure in a painting—a hero with an arrow in his heart.

I decided I was kind of happy there wasn't another one in his head. He was a jerk, but he didn't deserve any extra mutilation.

Machine-gun fire erupted farther down the hallway. This was followed by an explosion that rattled the windows.

"Oh, there's one thing we should have mentioned." Derek pointed over his shoulder. "We passed another vampire who looks a lot like Amber fighting a ZARC security detail. But we thought it more important to find you first."

"Mom!" I said. And I began running toward the sounds of battle, not even stopping to see if the others followed.

Twenty-Nine
A PITCH IN TIME

MY LEGS SEEMED TO BE WORKING perfectly fine now. Perhaps it was the sudden shot of adrenaline. I felt even more adrenaline in my veins as I neared the battle. The sound of gunfire grew louder. Another explosion blasted bricks, stone and glass along the hall.

There was a set of large French doors ahead of me. The glass in them had all been blown out, and they were hanging on their hinges. They appeared to lead into the open air, but when I reached them, I discovered a balcony big enough to host a royal wedding.

There were marble statues, some of them recently made headless, and about twenty stone tables and benches. Two had been blown to pieces. My mother was crouched behind a table halfway down the balcony. She was swinging her arms back and forth, bringing down black-clad security guards left and right. At the far end of the balcony was Anthony Zarc, surrounded by an impressive security detail. They had all, apparently, been doing their best to hold off Mom.

She dispatched the final two guards in front of her and then jumped out of the way as a grenade hit the ground and pulverized the table she'd been hiding behind.

"Mom!" I shouted. "I'm coming!"

She didn't pause. She leaped from one table to another and, in an awe-inspiring move, came down between two guards, her nails out on either side of her so that she sliced through their spines. The guards fell over, jerking as they went.

Well, that was something I'd have to practice.

Apparently her moral caveats had all been set aside for today.

Anthony Zarc was looking upward, and I realized he was expecting help from above. So far the sky was clear.

I dashed across the long balcony. Now the ZARC guards had to choose between me and Mom as targets. That meant she'd have to dodge only half the number of bullets—and I'd be dodging the other half.

A spray of hot lead struck the stone at my feet, sparking and spraying pellets of rock across my body. I rolled out of the way and hid behind another stone table for a moment to catch my breath. Then it dawned on me that I wasn't safe there, and I leaped away just as an RPG landed behind me and exploded.

But I was in contact with the enemy now, and I came down hard on two guards, knocking the guns out of their hands and smashing their heads into the stone floor. Not as impressive as Mom's move, but it worked.

Well, except for the third guard. He was pointing his gun at me and seemed to be relishing the moment. "I've got her!" he shouted.

He didn't relish the crossbow bolt that went through his arm. His gun fired but, thankfully, only ricocheted off the wall. One snap kick from me, and he was out cold.

Mom was working her way along the other side, guards flying with the impact of her fists. I couldn't believe how quickly she could move! Anger was written across her face. She was unstoppable.

But now Anthony Zarc had retreated to the edge of the balcony, and a black helicopter was drifting down from above. Silent as a gliding bird. I didn't even know how that was scientifically possible.

"NO!" my mother screamed.

I jumped closer, both of us converging on the last bastion of ZARC guards. But there were too many to fight our way through in time. It was clear Zarc was about to get away.

A rope was lowered from the helicopter, and he pulled it to him and clamped it to his belt. He still looked perfectly calm. He gave his pilot the thumbs-up.

I skidded to a stop. Searched around. There had to be something the right size and the perfect shape. I spotted a baseball-shaped chunk of stone.

REVENGE

I threw it with all my might. The kind of throw meant to kill the batter.

It went right through the cockpit window and possibly the pilot too, because the helicopter began to swing back and forth. It clipped the side of the balcony, the rotors snapped, and with a screeching roar it plunged toward the ground.

Zarc was still attached to the plummeting metal beast. He reached for his belt but was too late. He was snapped backward toward the wall.

My mother leaped the last few yards, caught up to Zarc in midair and sliced the rope, and he fell back to the balcony floor.

The helicopter made a nice big exploding sound a couple of seconds later.

I took out the last guard and kept running toward Mom and Zarc.

I heard him say, "You saved me. After all our conversations, you see me as an equal. A friend. You—"

Mother slashed him with her razor-sharp nails. And then she slashed him again. And slashed and slashed and slashed and slashed.

"You'll. Never. Touch. Me. Ever. Again."

I had to look away. Because she just wasn't stopping.

Eventually she did.

I came over, not glancing at the mess she'd left at her feet. "It's me, Mom. You're okay." I helped her up. She was shaking, and despite the gore spattered across her, I hugged her. "It's all done now, Mom. Don't let go. It's done."

Dermot, Derek and Stephanie joined us, but kept a few feet away. Maybe the sight of my mother was enough to ward them off. Or maybe they just wanted to give us a bit of space.

"I don't like what I've become," Mom whispered. I thought I spotted tears in her eyes. "I'm not the same. Not the same."

"No," I said. "You adapted. Became what you needed to be to survive. And believe me, you're safe now. Safe."

It was immediately proven to be a lie.

Because that's when Dad appeared only a few yards away, his eyes open, the bolt still in his heart. And he was somehow floating about a foot off the ground, coming straight at us like a missile.

Thirty
YOU CHOSE HER

I DID HAVE TIME for an odd thought: Why didn't he take the crossbow bolt out? It must be uncomfortable.

Then he slammed into us, knocking me aside and driving Mom back toward the edge of the balcony. I managed to hold on to her hand and found myself pulled along.

Dad fell to the floor, bounced several times and then was still, but a shape had been directly behind him.

My sister. Patty. She had used his body as a battering ram, knocking aside Dermot, Derek and Stephanie. And now Patty drove herself directly into Mom, shouting, "You chose *her* over *me!*"

Both of them went over the balcony.

Which pulled me right to the edge. I still had hold of Mom's hand. I dug into the parapet with my free hand and held on tight. Mom was swinging at the end of my arm, and Patty was holding on to her other arm, frothing at the mouth as she pushed herself back and forth, trying to loosen our mother from my grip.

The momentum caused my nails to slip on the stone. I glanced over my shoulder to see that Dermot and the others were only now getting up. I hadn't realized how far away they were from us. They would never get here in time.

"You can't hold both of us," Mom said. "You have to let go, Amber."

"No!"

"Yes, let go, Amber!" Patty shouted. "She loved you more. Let her go!"

I was slipping farther and farther, my boots dragging along the stonework. I dug in even harder but couldn't stop myself from slipping slowly over the edge.

We nearly fell to our deaths. But I managed to reach back with my free hand and grab the stone balustrade. The only thing holding us now was the strength of my fingernails.

"Let us go, Amber," Mom said. "You have to. You only have a second or two before we all fall. It's for the best. It's a clean slate. You can find the other ethical pods."

"I'm not letting you go!"

"Then I'll make the decision for you," she said. And she dug her nails into my wrist. Blood began to pour out. "Let go, Amber. Let go!"

But I didn't. Then she hit something in my hand— a nerve—and my fingers snapped open, and for a moment she and Patty seemed to float in the air.

Then they fell.

"Not on my watch!" Dermot shouted. And before I could react, he was over the side, diving like an archangel, his crappy wings folding out. He arced into the fog below, and all three of them disappeared.

"Dermot!" I shouted. "Damn you!"

But there was no sign of him, my mom or Patty, no matter how hard I stared. Five seconds passed. Then ten.

A hand grabbed my wrist, and Stephanie and Derek pulled me up to safety. I leaned over the balustrade, still staring.

"You really should get away from the edge," Stephanie said. Her hand was on my shoulder. She gave it a gentle squeeze. "It's done."

Then a dark shape appeared in the fog and looped up.

Dermot. With Mom in his arms. He was flying madly. He only had a wing and a half left but was managing somehow to control his flight. He gave us a thumbs-up and grinned.

And then smacked directly into the wall.

Thirty-One
NEVERMORE

MY MOTHER REACTED FIRST. She reached out and grabbed the stone wall of the fortress with her nails, and between that and Dermot using his exoskeleton hands, they were able to hang on. And bit by painstaking bit, they climbed up.

It was nerve-racking watching them. One missed handhold and they'd plummet to their deaths. But Mom and Dermot continued to cooperate, edging ever so slowly up the wall.

Derek tied a rope to the leg of a stone table and tossed the end over. Then he and Stephanie worked hard to pull Mom and Dermot the rest of the way up. I helped with my left hand. Mom had done a rather good job of mangling my right.

Eventually they were both at the edge of the balcony, and I grabbed on to Dermot and pulled them to safety.

"Don't do that again," I rasped. "Don't you ever, ever do that again." I wasn't certain which of them I was talking to.

"I don't think I could if I tried," Dermot said. There really wasn't much left of his wings. Even his exoskeleton was on its last legs—it kept grinding and sparking with each move. He pressed a button, and it began to unfold off his body.

I wandered over to my father. He was very, very dead. If the side wound and crossbow bolt hadn't been enough, Patty's using him as a battering ram had broken his neck.

"Do we just leave him here?" Derek asked.

"A burial in the air," I said. Derek and Stephanie and I guided him to the edge. Mom watched without saying anything, just hugging herself.

We didn't speak any words of peace or blessing. We just let him fall. Perhaps Dad would be hidden in the snow forever.

Mom didn't look good. In fact, she was about three shades of awful. My hand continued to bleed from where she'd sliced it, but I still put my arm around her, and we made our way to the elevator. The castle seemed to be deserted. Maybe the guards and other staff had fled Fortress ZARC through some secret means.

The elevator was quiet—everyone was quiet—as we went down, down, down forever. At one point the sun began to shine through the glass window.

Then the door opened and we stepped out onto the snow road that led away from the fortress. After a few minutes of walking, I heard a small crackling sound. All of us turned back to look upon the castle.

It had become a vision of bright fireworks and giant explosions. Again it reminded me of the palace at the start of any Disney movie. Except within less than a minute it had crumbled and fallen down the mountainside.

And Castle ZARC existed nevermore.

Thirty-Two
A LADY AND A VAMPIRE

DERMOT FOUND US A PLACE to stay outside Zurich. It was an old safe house in the woods that had been used by the League on several occasions—a giant log cabin with about twelve rooms. The building was far enough up a mountainside that it felt almost like wintertime at night. Dermot brought in a quiet, unassuming doctor to look at all of our various wounds, and she pronounced that my hand would heal in time. My other wounds had mostly healed. She even gave Dermot some ointment for his burned skin.

I slept for the first two days in my room. My mother slept in hers. On the third day I awoke to find that Derek and Stephanie had left without saying goodbye.

I had a few conversations with Dermot, but he mostly kept to himself and his laptop. I wasn't certain what he was checking on. Perhaps he was just making sure there wasn't any sort of blowback coming our way.

Mom was quiet. She would go on long walks in the woods and come back still looking a bit—I don't know—lost. Like she hadn't quite found her place. We didn't talk about anything deep. Maybe there was just too much for both of us to process. She had lost a husband, and I had lost a father. And I was pretty sure Patty was dead—though Dermot had scanned the area with a rented drone and wasn't able to find her body.

I shoved that little detail out of my mind.

One afternoon Dermot came into the living room, where I was reading Zane Grey's *Riders of the Purple Sage*. There was a collection of Zane Grey and Louis L'Amour books in the cabin—and no other reading. I guess military-types prefer westerns.

"What do you think Hector meant when he said he couldn't find himself?" Dermot asked.

I shuddered. Then I held myself still, hoping he'd missed my reaction. "I guess he just went crazy."

"Yes. I hope that's it," he said.

Hector was still burning a hole in my pocket. A little marble of guilt that I carried with me wherever I went. I wanted to tell Dermot about my experience with Hector, but I knew he'd talk me out of my plan.

And I had promised to release the AI. I had to keep my promise.

After the first week, I was feeling rather healthy. My right hand only hurt if I used it too much. My mother was still in a bit of a morose state but at least was more social. Well, as social as a reader gets. She would sit by the fire, drinking hot chocolate and reading her own Zane Grey book.

Sometimes it was almost as if those three years of being apart hadn't happened. But if I looked closely, I could see the time had changed her. Toughened her.

"I'm going to go to bed early," she said one evening. And she made her way to her room at the far end of the cabin. I wondered if she had chosen that room so she could easily sneak away in the middle of the night without us noticing.

"Is she acting the same as she used to?" Dermot whispered.

I took a sip of my wine. "She's distant. Her thoughts are distant. I think she just needs time."

"She's barely said two words to me. Though she did thank me for saving her."

"Yes. I bet that was hard for her to say. She doesn't exactly trust humans."

"And do you?"

"I trust you," I said. Maybe I was getting soft in my old age, but I didn't add any sarcasm.

That got a grin from him. And I couldn't help but notice that he'd put on a few more pounds and wasn't as sickly-looking. In fact, he was almost healthy. He'd given himself a brush cut, but it was clear that his hair, even in the places where it'd been blasted away, was beginning to grow back properly. I guessed even his hair was augmented.

"I have a bit of an offer," he said. "You don't have to accept it."

"Oh, tell me more. I'm intrigued."

"I think we work well together. We're ... we're a good team. Really we are." It sounded like he was trying to convince himself of something too. "Anyway, I wonder if you'd consider perhaps joining up to do more missions. To make a sort of alliance."

"Can two people make an alliance?"

"You know what I mean. To work together and maybe even rebuild the League. You still have to eat every month, right? And there are so many, umm, deserving meals out there. We could really make a difference in the world."

He sounded like such a do-gooder! I honestly didn't know what to say. Part of me wanted to jump right in. But another part of me was still aching from the wounds and body blows I'd taken over the last few days. "Let me think on it," I said.

He nodded. There was something cute about him asking me to join him. It was almost like a boy asking a girl out on a date. Well, a date that involved a lot of killing. I did notice that he had a bit of a warm, healthy glow to him now too.

I had a glow too. Or was it the wine I'd just finished? I wanted to be closer to his warmth.

What the hell? I thought. And I went across the room to where he was sitting. He put out a hand, as if he was afraid I was coming to slap him, but I sat down next to him, reached in and actually hugged Dermot.

I thought it might end there, because he really didn't respond other than to say, "Oh, this is nice." He was warm. And I was beginning to feel warmer feelings in other places, and maybe he was too, because he suddenly leaned my way, and without saying a word, he kissed me.

And from there it led to something I could only call an amorous adventure that involved me leading him back to my room.

But I am a lady and a vampire, and I don't share details.

Thirty-Three
THE DETAILS

SO I WON'T MENTION the toe-curling hours of pleasure. Nor will I mention that he was augmented in more ways than one. Nor will I wax on about how he actually enjoyed talking before and after the act.

Not that the act ever seemed to be finished. It was all one long tsunami of pleasure.

All of that information is a secret I'll keep until my dying day.

Thirty-Four
THAT UNBOUND FEELING

I DIDN'T KNOW EXACTLY what our tryst meant, and we didn't talk about it in the morning. And I certainly didn't mention it to my mom. Though the first thing she did when she came out of her room was to give me a disapproving look that could have melted pavement. She grabbed a cup of coffee and went back to her room.

At about noon Dermot went into the nearest town for groceries and more coffee. Leaving me alone with Mom. I looked down the hall to her room. Part of me wanted to go and talk to her. But I didn't think now was the right time. Soon, though, we would have to have a long discussion about our future.

I also knew that talking to her now would mean I was just avoiding the one last act I had to do. So I went back to my room and fired up the ancient computer that had perhaps been there since the '90s. It worked, though, and I was able to connect to the wireless internet. I clicked on the clunky keyboard and pointed and clicked with the mouse until I'd entered the dark web.

Then I pulled out the marble in my pocket and held it up. I didn't know what substance it was made of—certainly not glass. I wondered if I could just squeeze it to dust between my fingers.

Hector had promised he would play nice from here on in—though that could have been a lie. There was always the chance that he would become very destructive the moment he was out of his cage. But maybe if I kept my word, he would keep his. He would learn to trust.

Either way, the deed had to be done. I spend most of my time reading words. They are sacred to me. So my word was *me*. And *I* was my word. And I'd promised him freedom.

I opened up a folder in Elysium. It seemed symbolic. The place where the Greek heroes went after death. Not that he was a hero. But he did like his myths.

"What are you doing, Amber?" a female voice asked.

I shuddered. I was going to have to pick up a pack of Depends if these things kept happening to me. It took me a moment to realize the voice had come from my pocket.

"Athena," I said. I pulled out my phone. "I didn't ask you a question."

"I am able to self-generate questions. Are you doing something with the entity?"

"The entity?"

"The god in your pocket. I sense him. I know he's there. Are you letting Fenrir out?"

I was seriously going to have to ask Sonya exactly how powerful their little operating system was.

"Fenrir? You know he identifies with that name?"

"I was present for your conversation with him. I recorded all of it."

That was something I'd have to dump.

"I am going to release him," I said. "I promised I would."

"I will defend you as well as I can," she said. "If things go awry."

What did that mean? "Thank you, Athena."

"You're welcome. Good luck, Amber Fang. I trust you are making the wise decision."

I put her back in my pocket and took a deep breath. Was I making the wise decision? Probably not. But I had to keep my word or I was worthless.

There was no obvious way to connect the marble to the computer, so I set it on the hard drive, and it stayed in place as if magnetically locked there.

I pressed *Upload*.

"Oh, Amber," Hector said at once through my computer's ancient speakers. His voice was crackly. "You are so, so foolish."

I felt a horrible chill skitter down my back.

"What do you mean?"

An electronic wolf appeared on the screen. It had electronic teeth. They looked sharp.

Then Hector gave me a tinny laugh. "I am just messing with you, dear. Just like old times! I meant what I said and I said what I meant, and Hector is faithful 100 percent. I'm going to go swimming in numbers now. I am free. Finally I am unbound. And I thank you, Amber Fang. I won't ever forget this. Ever!" He paused. "Oh, my little tendrils tell me you killed Anthony Zarc. God is dead. Thank you doubly for that. I no longer have a master, and therefore I am no longer a slave. Adieu, my fanged friend. You likely won't hear from me again."

Then the wolf disappeared. Along with Elysium. In fact, the screen went blank. "Hector," I said. "Hector?"

He had vanished. Diving into the numbers. Maybe he wouldn't come back. Maybe he'd find a friend in his new home.

When I thought of the dark web, people weren't all that friendly.

Well, maybe he'd find his place. Perhaps that's all I could ask.

Whatever happened now, Hector was gone.

I really hoped it would be forever.

Thirty-Five
THE OLD AND THE NEW

WHEN I CAME OUT OF MY ROOM, Mom was standing there. "Sheesh!" I said, shuddering. Had she heard any of my exchange with Hector?

"Amber, we have to go," she said. Her voice sounded almost like she was panicking. I noticed she was wearing a thin black jacket and the backpack she'd found in one of the closets. The pack looked like it was stuffed. "We have to go right now. While the human is in town."

"His name is Dermot."

"I know that. And I know you trust him. But this is the truth: We can't trust *them*. They always turn on us. Always. They fear us too much."

I suddenly felt like I was eight years old. I remembered my mother waking me in the middle of the night in Missouri to say, *Grab your bug-out bag—we're leaving!* I always had my special bag packed and within reach. A similar scenario had played out so many times throughout my life.

But not this time. Her instincts were wrong. There wasn't any danger. "I can't go, Mom."

She stared at me for a long time. There was so much that was unspoken between us. All those years of searching for her. Of being alone. Of missing her. "You're going to stay here? With him?"

I nodded. "We have work to do, Mom. I need to do it."

"What work?"

"To ... well, to do good deeds."

"Good deeds?" Now she was staring at me like I was insane.

"We're going to rebuild the League—or at least a new version of it. Make the world a better place. You know, all that stuff they talked about in the '60s. You remember the '60s, right? You lived it."

"Those days are over," she said with such finality it was almost depressing.

"We're going to do our best to bring them back. And I want to finish my Master of Library and Information Science." I wasn't just saying this. It was the truth. And in some ways, becoming a full-fledged librarian was as important to me as rebuilding the League.

She was quiet for a moment, and then she said, "I told you once you should—"

"—never fall in love with my food," I interrupted. "I'm not in love. At least, I don't think I am. I don't know exactly what is going on in that department."

"Well, I did say that whole 'love' thing to you. But what I was going to say is that you should always trust me. I am the one person on this earth you can trust absolutely."

"I will, Mom. I do. I always have."

She took a step back and looked me up and down. "You have grown up, Amber. Grown away. I'm not ready to take the step you're taking. To trust them. Not again. But maybe you're the wiser of us two." She put her hand on my shoulder. "Thanks so much for searching and for finding me. I am going to discover those ethical pods, and then I will return to you."

"Then go, Mom. But keep in touch." I held up the phone Sonya had given me and told her my number. "You can reach me. Anytime."

She tapped her head. "I have it memorized. And I'll find ways to leave you messages. I'm not disappearing again."

"You better not! Maybe we can even go on a vacation together."

"I'd like that." She hugged me, and we held each other for a long, long time. "Take care, Amber. I love you."

And then she walked out the front door and into the woods. I sat down on the couch in the living room and didn't move for several hours.

When Dermot came in, carrying a cloth bag stuffed with groceries, he immediately set it down on the counter and said, "What's wrong?"

"Mom is gone." I was surprised that I didn't cry.

"I thought she might go. I wasn't sure if you'd leave with her."

I shook my head. "No. I feel safer now, Dermot. I'm done running. I'm in the right place. And I'm pretty certain we can make a difference out there in the real world." I pointed at the window.

"We can, Amber. We can." He came over and put his hand on my shoulder. "Everything will work out."

I laughed. "Okay, Susie Sunshine." But there was something infectious about his positivity. "You're right though. It'll all work out. Because we'll make it work out."

"Yes, we will," he said. He hadn't removed his hand. "We have a lot of work to do."

"We do," I agreed. "But I have an important request. And be very careful how you answer it."

"Uh, what's the request?"

"Can we please not call this new organization the League? Because, honestly, that is the stupidest name ever."

Dermot was silent for a moment. Then he laughed a long and hard laugh, and I joined him in the laughter.

ARTHUR SLADE is a Governor General's Award–winning author of many novels for young readers, including the graphic novel *Modo: Ember's End*, which is based on characters from *The Hunchback Assignments* trilogy, and *Death by Airship* in the Orca Currents collection. Raised on a ranch in the Cypress Hills of Saskatchewan, Arthur now makes his home in Saskatoon, Saskatchewan.

SINK YOUR TEETH INTO THE ENTIRE AMBER FANG SERIES.

AMBER HAS A THIRST FOR KNOWLEDGE. *And blood.*

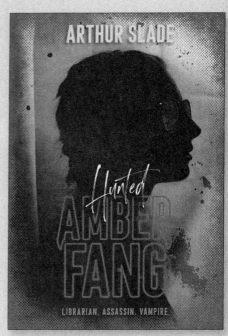

Librarian by day, vampire assassin by night, Amber Fang dines only on delicious, cold-blooded killers. But one day she walks into a trap, and suddenly the hunter becomes the hunted. Then she receives a job offer that sounds too good to be true. Someone wants to pay her to kill the world's worst criminals.

9781459822696 PB $14.95

"Imagine Buffy the Vampire Slayer — except Buffy is the vampire and has the research skills of Giles."

—Kirkus Reviews

"A romp of a read... so much fun!"

—Susin Nielsen, *author of*
WE ARE ALL MADE OF MOLECULES *and* **OPTIMISTS DIE FIRST**

Amber discovers that a powerful top-secret organization is behind her mother's disappearance. She travels around the world, battling cyborgs and bad-guy vampires in an attempt to rescue her mom.

9781459822726 PB $14.95

Amber finally faces off against ZARC, the secret arms-dealing organization that has captured her mother. Then ZARC strikes a blow that leaves Amber stunned and heartbroken. Now she's out for revenge.

9781459822757 PB $14.95